Bot Diaries

Copyright © 2020 Dennis Patrick Treece

ISBN (Hardcover): 978-1-989942-04-8
ISBN (Paperback): 978-1-989942-03-1
ISBN (Ebook): 978-1-989942-05-5
Printed in the United States of America

ELK PRESS
Great Books... Great Times.

ELK PRESS
112th Street, Suite 904 Edmonton, AB T5K 2J1 Canada
www.elkpress.ca
+1 888 410 0122

Dedication

This book is dedicated to all the dreamers out there who will bring these diaries to life in their own minds and in their own ways. Enjoy!

Forward

Young, pre-adult Shonakian students learn about Earth near the end of their 40-year formal education. In order to understand and enjoy a lifetime of Earther vid-watching they must understand Earther behavior and how Earthers came to behave the way they do. These young Shonakian students also need to understand just what the vid-collecting bot fleet is capable of. Products from bot collection are known as Bot Diaries.

In the Solar Rotation 306761/3 Eldest, Grand Team Education and Training requested vid examples of Earther behavior which will form the basis of their formal education on the subject. The students are in the fourth quarter of their forty-year education, and are located in more than twenty-two hundred education centers across all 142 of Shonak's administrative regions. At the conclusion of these lectures they will be given access to a library of selected historical vids chosen for their educational value.

GT Eldest thought it proper to introduce Earther behaviors to this worldwide audience of senior students in an academic setting before they see this behavior in any unrestricted vids. Previous generations had commented that they could have benefitted from some educational frame of reference in order to fully understand what they were seeing. Their Vid-Watch clubs filled this void for the young red dots eventually but not as efficiently as standardized formal education.

The student versions of these diaries contain the accompanying videos but in this written version the videos are unavailable.

Table of Contents

- Welcome Introduction   10
  by Eldest, GT Education and Training

- Opening Lecture   23
  by Eldest of Curriculum, GT Education and
  Training: Contrasting Earther and Shonak
  Behavior

- Diary Number One: Establishing Expectations   33
  – Introducing Basic Earther Behavior Norms

- Diary Number Two: Earther Social Injustice   49
  – Social Class Divisions

- Diary Number Three: Specific Historical   75
  Question
  - Who Named Alexander The Great's Horse?

- Diary Number Four: Clarifying History   89
  – Cleopatra's Final Secrets

- Diary Number Five: Witnessing Inventiveness   101
  – The Bow and Arrow

- Diary Number Six: Witnessing Inventiveness   110
  - The Stirrup

- Diary Number Seven: Solving Mysteries   125
  – The Lost Colony of Roanoke

- Diary Number Eight: Following Objects Over   146
  Time
  – Thirty Pieces of Silver

- Diary Number Nine: Humbot Influencing a   177
  Famous Earther
  – Wolfgang Amadeus Mozart

- Diary Number Ten: Information Integrity   183
  – How Shonak Helped Earth Overcome The
  Assault on Truth

- Diary Number Eleven: Influencing Earther   191
  Myths and Legends

- Diary Number Twelve: In Search of the Soul   208

Welcome Introduction by Eldest, Grand Team Education and Training

Welcome to the final decade of your formal education. Since you hatched thirty Solar Rotations ago we have introduced you to our planet, Shonak. In the first ten Solar Rotations you learned our language, system of weights and measures, our geography, our astronomy, and our history. In the second ten S-Rots you learned our math and science. In the third quarter you learned our technology and how we are organized as a global mono-culture with our system of Grand Teams and Regions, and age-based system of elders and Eldests. You have been schooled in the workings of all the Grand Teams that maintain our planet. The food we eat, the roads we use, the power we consume, the manufacturing of all our technology, the technology itself, our arts and our transportation and medicine, pure science and exploration. As a result of what you now know of our culture you understand what is expected of you over your very long lives and how to behave in concert with your teammates and fellow citizens; hard work, dedication to team missions, maintenance and advancement of our peaceful culture. Looking back at it, you will see that up to now your education has been an inward look at Shonak and what it means to be a Shonakian.

In this final quarter of your education we will broaden your horizons. We are now introducing you to what lies beyond ourselves.

Shonak is not alone. We exist in a complex

cosmology of physical universes which are similar but not exact copies of each other. There are six solar systems in our physical space which contain six similar but not exact copies of each other. We are separated by our native resonant frequencies, or natural vibrations. Each of the six universes has these six different native resonances. We know this because after we discovered phase technology, we visited these five other worlds. We now call this our resonant family of planets. Shonak occupies the slowest of the six physical planetary vibrations and we call this the Prime Vibration. The five planets above us are named Plus-One through Plus-Five to denote their different native resonance. In the case of Plus-One and Plus-Five we refer to them by the name their natives have chosen. The dominant intelligent species on Plus-One calls their planet "Home". The dominant intelligent species on Plus-Five calls their planet "Earth". When referring to the native frequency or resonance of these planets we use the Plus-One and Plus-Five designations. When referring to the planets, we use the names given them by their own people.

The six planets themselves are physically similar but not identical. Plus-One/Home is very much like Shonak in appearance and climate and has two intelligent life forms; one just emerging and one very advanced but less advanced than ourselves. The population of these intelligent life forms is small. Plus-Two was until recently an arid world, devoid of water when Emerald Bon asked GT Exploration to punch through the crust to get at the water underneath. It now resembles Shonak in most respects except it has only microscopic life forms, both plant and animal. Plus-Three resembles Shonak in most ways except that it only has plant life; no animal life at all. Plus-Four is the most divergent of these six planets. To begin with, it has no moon. We believe the moon fell to Earth and the collision caused both bodies to be consumed in plasma fires which have not yet cooled. It is totally volcanic with no life of any kind and little surface water. Its planetary supply of water is thought to equal ours but is mostly trapped in the hot air of the planet which has a very dense atmosphere. The water is in an endless cycle of falling as rain only to be heated back into steam again and raising back into the atmosphere. Its gravity is stronger due to its greater mass and one day we will enjoy studying it further, but that time is perhaps millions of S-Rots in the future. We have no idea when it will be cool enough and stable enough to visit. At the top of the resonant spectrum we have Plus-Five/Earth. It is very much like Shonak in its geography and weather but that is where the similarities end. We will teach you about the other planets in more detail later but we will now introduce you to Earth in some detail so you can understand the historical vids from that planet you will shortly have access to.

Earthers are very different from Shonakians. They have a very diverse, very complex sociology and history and Shonakians have derived a great deal of entertainment from watching them go about their very different, very active lives while their cultures have matured. They are not only different from us in appearance and conduct but are also different in many ways from each other. Unlike our monoculture, theirs is extraordinarily diverse.

You will become devoted to vid-watching

Earthers but because of the Law of Nativity you will never be able to visit Earth without phase shifting technology. The Law of Nativity holds that all physical matter resonates at the vibration it was born into and cannot be changed. So we can't live on the other five worlds and they cannot live on Shonak. But we can enjoy each other's company, in a manner of speaking.

Because we derive so much interest from watching the lives of the humans on Earth, we determined to saturate their planet with surveillance devices of many different types to ensure we capture all the audio and video from every scene . We call the surveillance collection devices "bots". They are made of Earth-native materials because of the Law of Nativity. If they were made of Shonak materials, they would need resonance changing equipment to keep them from reverting to our own resonance. That would render them easily detectable by the people there. The resonance equipment we use causes things to appear blurry and gives off a distinct humming sound. Earth natives find both to be very annoying and it makes some of them sick to be near them. As a result, we only field bots made of materials native to the resonance where they are deployed. On Earth we have a maintenance and manufacturing facility deep under their Sahara Desert. There are no doors to this facility. Everything phases into it and out again leaving no signs of passage. Earthers are not aware of this facility and we are careful to keep it that way. All bots are controlled by Bot Control under the Infotainment Grand Team working closely with Grand Team Plus-Five/Earth. Humbot Control is the Team which controls the construction and placement and maintenance of humbots, but it is the Vid-Watch clubs that determine when and where a humbot is needed. Indeed, the Vid-Watch clubs essentially determine the placement and priorities for collection of all bots, both static and dynamic.

Most of these collection devices, these bots, resemble natural things on Earth, like rocks, trees, birds, small animals or even insects, which we do not have here on Shonak. We also use native human-appearing bots to achieve the level of interactive vid-collection our people demand. These human bots, which we refer to as humbots, are like Earthers in every detail, and constitute some of our greatest technological achievements. While we have cultivated an open relationship with the people of Earth it remains for us essentially a zoo or cultural theme park to watch at our leisure. We have told them about our interest in them and that we enjoy watching some of their public activities but we have never told them just how intrusive or extensive our bot fleet is. In return, we do provide them with vids of a number of our public facilities so they can feel we are reciprocating but they have no idea how much of their lives we have access to and we do not intend for them to find out. During the time of Emerald OE Bon, one of our humbots was discovered after it malfunctioned, and this caused great anger on Earth. We publicly destroyed more than a million bots as a result of their outrage and we had no open communication with them for one hundred S-Rots. OE Bon re-established good relations with them after that time and told them all humbots would from that time forward only be fielded at their request and would not look so human as to fool anyone. What Bon did not tell them was that we secretly kept fifty thousand of the "perfect" humbots in place and we have not told them about the tens of thousands we have introduced since. These bots can anti-grav or phase out of any situation and none of them has been discovered since that one unfortunate incident back in Shonak 306210, Earth 2373 UAY.

The dramatic differences between our two worlds is what makes vid-watching so popular. With nothing to do on Shonak but work for the common good, when we do find time away from our teams it has become the norm to watch our favorite Plus-Five characters and their scenarios playing out in real time. We have formed clubs devoted to both general or specific Earther things of interest. One might watch a particular king and his court or a struggling family in a poor remote village somewhere, or military operations or a night of jazz music in a night club on Earth. One person might focus on their struggle with rudimentary tools and another might follow their use of engineering forms in architecture. Many of us are more interested in their distant past, before technology and mass communications, but others prefer their high-tech present. There are tens of thousands of these Vid-Watch clubs on Shonak, all devoted to their own interests and all clamoring for more coverage by the Plus-Five Infotainment Team that builds, maintains and places purpose-built surveillance bots at their request.

Before we begin with all that it is essential that you understand more about how Shonak monitors Earther activity. There are two basic types of bots; static and mobile. Static bots are helpful in places where coverage of video and audio can be achieved without moving the sensor. Static bots come in many forms but all are camouflaged to appear part of the landscape if outside or part of the building if inside. These devices can be very small without losing their ability to generate high quality visual and audio output. They operate in low light and no light situations and maps of their locations are available in the various Vid-Watch clubs or on comm with Grand Team Plus-Five. Eldest, GT Plus-Five welcomes requests for additional static sensor placement to facilitate better viewing by Vid-Watch clubs.

Mobile bots are in the form of insects, small and large birds, animals and Earthers. They have the ability to move about and improve collection on people and situations that are themselves dynamic. A bird flying over a scene or a person actually participating in it can collect much more imagery from one or more angles. Multiple bots covering a single scene provide the best chance for optimal coverage.

Each bot has a unique identifier which allows the Vid-Watch clubs to see what each can do, where it is, and what it is currently doing. Most Vid-Watch clubs "own" their own bot fleets and keep close watch on their status and collection . They can watch what they collect in real-time or review archives of what they have already collected. Some historical research projects require the combined fleets of many Vid-Watch clubs and members take great pride in their ability to seamlessly follow a subject from one team's bots to the next. Many of the examples of bot collection demonstrate how well we can achieve continuity from one bot to the next or among multiple bots. This applies equally to live action or historical views.

It is also possible for a Vid-Watch effort to take control of bots from many different clubs and determine their collection location and priorities in furtherance of a specific, ongoing, real-time project.

The fleet of Shonakian humbots that have taken up covert residence on Plus-Five in order to watch and collect live vid-streams for the viewing pleasure of all Shonak has steadily expanded over time. Vid watching has also greatly expanded and Shonakian elders keep a close watch on us for any indication of Earther behavior developing among us on Shonak from all this exposure. Only two changes have been observed; there has been some encroachment by Plus-Five languages into our own, and more of our leisure time has been devoted to watching Earther vids. That is a welcome relief. And it must be pointed out that our Elders have no such concerns for the reverse effect. In fact, we feel Earth could only benefit if some of their behavior was more like our own.

Our humbots are interacting daily with Earthers and of course they are altering history for them in so many ways. The humbots are not there to alter history on Plus-Five but any and every time one of our humbots interacts with an Earther it will have some impact on its life and the things it is doing. Our Eldests have always reasoned that life everywhere is chaos anyway, so what does another cog in that wheel really mean in the overall scheme of things? There are, as a result, no prohibitions on humbot behavior as they work either independently or with Earther humans in pursuit of their Vid-Watch club objectives. They do need to be careful, however in order to avoid detection. For example, they must protect themselves from great injury that would show them to be machines. They are free to kill or maim Earther combatants as the case may arise if it keeps them from being damaged or even compromised. They are discouraged from becoming soldiers, though, and for example, because it is too difficult to keep their identities a secret in that environment. This could be either through observed super-human powers or by having an arm chopped off in combat with no bleeding or pain.

As Earth history progressed and their technology advanced it became more difficult to keep our bots of all kinds from being discovered. I refer here to any of them, not just the ones that look like people. There are large teams of Shonakians monitoring the entire Earth bot fleet and they take action whenever there is any danger of discovery. A tree-bot which serves as a collector in a village or some other desirable location must some day die, like all trees do. Typically, the people there will chop off the branches to keep them from falling on someone and eventually the tree is cut down. Or they cut it down for firewood. This is always a problem and our bot maintenance and security teams work continuously to ensure that they remove potential disclosures before they are discovered and examined. It is also essential to ensure that the entire fleet is updated to reflect the growing technological capabilities of the locals. A bird bot that collects aerial images may be shot down by a hunter and therefore compromise the entire operation so they must fly higher, change direction to avoid the projectile, or be taken out of service. Over the millennia this has become something of a game with the Shonakians staying one step ahead of the ever larger and more technically adept Earther population.

Of course, we see our humbot fleet as a triumph of our technological prowess, especially the ones designed to look, sound, and act in every way "human" on Earth. Living "Earther" is always a challenge, even for an automated being like a Shonakian bot fashioned to impersonate an Earth-native human. Care is taken to avoid "perfection" in appearance or in abilities. Often the humbots are in fact designed to be lame, ugly, dim-witted, so as to avoid a great deal of interest by real people. Their main purpose is to gather video that is both informative and entertaining for our professional and home audiences.

In the earliest days of Shonakian presence on Earth it was less of a risk for us and our humbots to mingle openly with the population. We made visits to Plus-Five in our shimmering phase suits and phase ships which would have looked other-worldly to the Earthers, and no few legends about gods and faerie folk and space ships emerged from these visits. Our overt visits gradually tapered off as the Earthers became more populous, educated, and scientific. Open visitation using phase equipment was to a large extent replaced by native-resonant machines. The humbots were designed to interact with the natives in order to collect more informative and entertaining vids and even to stimulate activity which the watchers on Shonak found to their liking. The various consumers of the videos here, our Vid-Watch clubs, would make requests in real time to "their" humbots to elicit information or to stimulate some sort of action they wanted to see. Once again, the product of any bot, whether human-looking or not, is known as a Bot Diary.

Once the natives had developed their sciences to the point where personal identity was checked against family history and biometric information, it was necessary for us to construct our humbots with the characteristics designed to pass the most rigorous of the Earther identification schemes. We monitor this technology closely to anticipate their advances in this area so we can prepare our humbot fleet in advance. Our humbots today also need not only the physical manifestations of identity but also the social and family backgrounds, family histories. These things are all achievable under Shonakian science and in fact, our teams responsible for designing and building these complex bots take great pride in the perfection they have achieved. The final aspects of humbot creation and fielding lay in the language or languages they speak, the clothing they wear, the occupations they pursue, the appearance and the "health" of their humbots, and their personalities. They are provided with a sense of humor, appropriate fight/flight responses, the ability to eat and drink, and the ability to act out the lies of life with finesse and accuracy. They also need to think on their feet with the ability to make instant decisions that match their cover stories. Their base programs are all the same but each humbot is in a different social situation and that requires flexibility of thought to act appropriately and convincingly at all times. They need to sleep, to be sick from time to time, to get drunk, to have a hangover, to have accidents and sustain injury, to get mad, to be sad, to be kind or cruel, all of the things Earthers do and feel and say are what the humbots must do, too.

In addition to being perfectly "Earther", which means perfectly flawed along the lines of "human nature", all Shonakian humbots have had the ability to change their phase of resonance and they also had anti-grav flight. When necessary they can phase away from their "lives" and fly to the bot maintenance facility in the remote desert undetected by even the most sensitive of Earth's modern military sensors. In that facility they are provided the things they need to continue their successful function. They are "aged" as needed, repaired if necessary, given new power packs, and other things like the ability to speak another language or learn another skill. They may have even died in their life in one place and are then prepared for life in another.

Given the numbers of them we have there at present it is not very inaccurate to say our bots of all types record every moment of every human action across the globe.

The Earth Calendar referenced in your educational examples use Earth's Universally Accepted Year (UAY) in spite of the fact that most of the times covered either had no calendar or used older versions. The UAY calendar was adopted by the Earth World Government following their last nuclear war. Their historically endless religious, secular and nationalistic wars highlighted their need to see themselves as a single culture, much like the Shonakians see themselves. Like us they live on a single planet, albeit with different histories and races and languages and religions and diets and all the rest, so it is better to get along with each other than continuously look for reasons to fight. A universally implemented calendar seemed a good example that at some time world solidarity could actually be achieved. This has not yet happened.

The following course of instruction is designed to prepare you for the limited number of vids from Earth you will shortly have access to. When you receive your red dots and enter Shonak society as an adult and join a Grand Team you will of course have permission for unlimited viewing. The diaries we have selected for you are not presented in chronological order. Rather, they are presented in the sequence we feel will best enable you to learn of Earth human behavior and thinking in all its forms, from the very basic to the most esoteric.

Opening Lecture by Eldest of Curriculum,

GT Education and Training - Contrasting Earther and Shonak Behavior

Just as we Shonakians recognize that we have no faults, Earthers have long recognized that they do. A popular Earther list has them reduced to the "seven deadly sins" but it can easily be argued they have more than seven. GT Eldest has decided to present these faults to you, which are also their differences from us. He wants you to see them from a Shonakian perspective in order to recognize our unique Shonakian frame of reference. We have no vested interest in them improving their conduct, but we do need to know them well enough to understand why they do certain things.

Before you begin your lifetime of viewing of life on Earth it is important that you understand how very different Earthers are from us. Let's begin with the physical differences. You can see in the picture here that, like us, they are also bipedal with two arms in something of the same proportions as we have. They are much larger than we are with on an average of nine times the weight and body mass of a Shonakian. While we are of no sex they are male and female and reproduce by copulation with the male fertilizing the female's egg which develops inside her body. After some 270 Planetary Rotations the female delivers a live baby, with no shell. This baby is totally helpless for many Solar Rotations and requires constant attention. The survival rate of newborns has increased greatly over time but in the beginning many children and their mothers died in the birth process. The dynamic of mating and childbirth has had a great influence on the family and societal structure and behavior of Earther humans.

Here you see a vid of people of different races. Unlike here on Shonak, where we all are nearly identical, Earthers have many different types of their species and even within these different types, black, brown, white, yellow, there are many different sub-species. These differences also have had significant impact on their behavior.

The planet itself has also had a tremendous influence on their lives and behaviors. It is a hostile world with many species that kill and eat both themselves and others. Not only do humans pose a danger to themselves but there are meat eating animals who feed on humans when they can, as well as poisonous plants and small beings called insects that are poisonous. The many dangers posed to the people of Earth has resulted in the evolution of survivor specialists who are quick to respond and consider all others a threat to their survival until proven otherwise. They call this their "fight or flight" response. They must decide instantly whether to run from danger or meet it and remove the threat by whatever means. Here on Shonak we favor placid behavior since there are no natural threats to our survival. On Earth it is aggressive and even violent behavior that has gotten them through the dark and dangerous early days of their existence. We also see a great deal of loving behavior between them, especially associated with the mating rituals they have, and family love, but every person who can show love can also show hate and violence. It is just their nature.

Here you see a typical male and a female Earther

human. They have body hair, they secrete water through their skin to keep cool, they are not cold-blooded like we are, but rather generate body heat through the process of digestion of their food and must keep their bodies within a certain temperature range for not only comfort but also survival. As you might imagine, bodies this large require a great deal of food and water, and they eat and drink whenever and wherever they can. They have the ability to taste their food, unlike Shonakians, which has allowed them to identify harmful things they should not eat. It has also led to a great deal of fussiness over their food. They have developed food preparation into a great art as well as science.

Not only are there anatomical differences but they also respond differently to external stimulation. The male of the species, you can see on the left, is larger and more muscular. They are more able to hunt and kill the animals on which they feed. The female is smaller and as the bearer of their children tends to be the more responsible of the two. On Shonak their propensity for harmful behavior would not be tolerated and indeed, none of their young would be allowed to hatch, even, given their tendencies to violence and other forms of anti-social behavior. But on Earth, it was the ones who fought back against the hostilities of their planet that survived and who passed on their aggressive tendencies to the next generations. Simply stated, peaceful planet Shonak has resulted in peaceful Shonakians and violent Earth has resulted in violent Earthers. Fortunately, there has been no evidence of Shonakian emulation of Earther behavior in the many thousands of S-Rots we have been watching the violent behavior of our Cousins up there.

We want to underscore this point. Unlike Shonak, Earthers evolved on a violent, hostile planet which required them to be defensive in nature and respond violently to threats in order to survive. They have faced attacks by wild animals and other humans. They have had to learn what foods will poison them, what animals and insects are harmful to them, which of them are good to eat, and which provide useful furs for warmth. This is instructive. On Shonak, there are no poisonous plants so we never needed to taste our vegetation to determine if it is safe to eat. Earthers learned by dying or getting sick which foods were healthy and which were not and their sense of taste helped them do that. The people with the most efficient taste buds lived and passed these better taste capabilities to the next generation while those who could not distinguish bad foods did not contribute as much to their gene pool and poor taste buds eventually died out. The same can be said for those with the most effective survival traits in all regards. We do find it interesting that they can express great love and tenderness as well as hatred and violence and can switch between them in the space of a single heartbeat when challenged or threatened.

Earthers are in competition for everything. The best food, the most desirable mate, more money, the most comfortable dwelling, and to be strongest, fastest, smartest, most successful and most powerful. The more power they have over the people around them and over their environment, the better chance they think they have for safety, security, and maintenance of the most comfortable life.

Political entities known as towns, cities, provinces, countries or nations are important on Earth, where societies are not monolithic, like they are here. We have one race, one culture and one language and no government. They have had many governments and still do but now they do have a world government, with an official world language, but the planet is still made up of hundreds of historical member countries, with sometimes dozens of languages spoken in each one. They have different modes of dress, different foods and beverages, different religions, different histories, different appearances and different races.

We know that our interest in all things Earthers do is fueled by the significantly different behavior between them and us. These differences are manifest in every aspect of life. For example, every day we eat one small, edible food tube of vegetable matter and water. That sustains us perfectly. We never cease to be amazed by, and love to watch, the many meals Earthers eat during their day. Not only do Earthers eat a variety of food and drink, in massive quantities, they never seem to stop, when food or drink is available. Other differences are just as striking. Shonakians have no religion or thought of religion but are fascinated by the diverse way in which Earthers pray and worship their gods. We think it should occur to them that if there were one, true religion, they would all be practicing it. But that is not the case. Another striking feature about Earth is their dependence on money for living. We Shonakians have no money, and no commerce, in our cashless society. You will find it amazing how much time and attention Earthers expend in the acquisition of wealth and the things they do to get more money and keep what they have, or to steal it if they don't. The list of differences goes on. Shonakians are of a single gender and produce eggs twice in our more than fifteen-hundred year lifetimes. Earthers, as mentioned earlier, are of two genders and they reproduce via the copulation of a male and female. In fact, almost all the plants and animals on Earth have these two genders and reproduction only takes place when they merge their gender-specific life forces. You will derive much viewing interest by the things Earthers do to win and keep sexual partners, mostly for breeding but also for pleasure, dominance, or economic advantage. Yet another difference; Shonakians have no politics at any level so we are fascinated by the amount of time Earthers devote to "getting ahead" or "taking charge" of anything and everything, from a family to a clan to a village to a city or to a kingdom, or even to an idea. The list of differences is almost endless. They have different human races and there is a great deal of discomfort, anger, and even bloodshed among them purely because of their differences and the perceived superiority of one over the other. They have crime, which involves such things as killing each other or stealing from each other, or cheating each other. Of course, we have none of that. Shonakians are never jealous of anyone but on Earth jealousy is common and leads to a great deal of destructive behavior. Earthers will set fire to another's home or business for a variety of reasons to include mental illness. And of course, Shonakians have no illnesses of any kind so these things will confound and confuse you at first as you watch Earthers go about their lives.

Earthers devote considerable time and energy to the production of beverages they enjoy tasting, and some of these beverages contain alcohol which causes them to become inebriated and behave differently, get sick, and sometimes even die from drinking too much. Eating and drinking to excess results in all manner of medical problems on Earth. In addition to the sickness caused by too much food or drink Earthers are also prone to sickness caused by microscopic pathogens called viruses and bacteria, as well as genetic problems. We are fortunate on Shonak that we have no such issues. Earthers also have keen senses of hearing and they have created music via many different instruments and electronics to make sounds they enjoy. Our great thinkers have often wondered why we never developed musical arts along with our sciences but we did not. Not all of us enjoy listening to their music but many do and of course you may listen to it any time you like once you are granted access. Their enjoyment of music is not the only dramatic art they have developed. They enjoy acting out various human tragedies and comedies and musicals to both celebrate and expose the light and dark sides of Earther nature. We have no equivalent to their dramatic arts here on Shonak but take some pleasure in watching theirs. They are also prolific artists, illustrating with thick liquids they call paint, that show a wide range of subjects and Earthers derive a great deal of satisfaction, as well as spend a good bit of their time, in the creation, sales, acquisition, and display of their static art.

Earthers live short lives, compared to Shonakians, with one hundred years, or Solar Rotations, being the upper limit for most of them. The shortness of their lives brings with it impatience to get things done and achieve self-imposed measures of success, before ill health or old age renders them unable to continue. Perhaps because of their short lives, and their many flaws, age does not automatically equate to wisdom or seniority, unlike here. People become "in charge" of others on Earth through various forms of selection and only rarely is age a factor. To them, "seniority" refers mostly to how long a person has been with a certain organization as well as to their position in it. For them success is the normal way to achieve leadership positions but it can also come about through family connections, buying it, or on the death of a leader. As a consequence, there is a great deal of effort expended by Earthers in an attempt to get promoted to higher positions that pay more money and confer more power. You will quickly come to see the wisdom of our completely uncompetitive system when you see the violence and overall turmoil in organizations and families and governments as people there fight to be "the boss".

Earthers have families, unlike us, and these families are historically important in the care of their new born since their babies are totally helpless for many S-Rots after birth. Earther young grow slowly, compared to us, and are not what we would call survivably independent until they are past ten S-Rots of age. Their family structures are complex and important throughout their lives.

Not surprisingly, what Earthers call "human nature" defines the way they behave. Competition in all things with money as the medium of exchange is woven together to describe all aspects of their short lives. We have no money on Shonak nor anything like it but on Earth money is their fundamental medium of exchange.

When they need or want something, they use money to achieve it, or "buy" it as they would say. People who work for their living are paid money with which to buy things, from food to transportation to clothing to education to leisure. Everything they cannot make themselves they must buy or trade for. Bartering is the trading of work or a thing for something else or vice versa. One Earther gives another a loaf of bread, and in return receives half a day of labor. That sort of thing. Bartering was a large part of the early Earther culture but has faded in popularity as more people there today have money. There are three basic ways to acquire money; work for it, have it given to you by your family, or steal it.

Crime is unknown on Shonak but it is prevalent on Earth. They have developed a complex criminal justice system that codifies criminal activity and assigns certain punishments for crimes but not all crimes are codified. On Shonak we would consider lying, for example, to be a crime but on Earth it is so prevalent it is only a crime when lying on some sort of official document or in some official proceeding. Shonak helped Earth reduce its criminal population by assisting them to capture their criminals and corrupt politicians and government officials and put them on a remote island to separate them from law abiding society. This program continues to the present, it is called Operation Purge and the criminals are sent to CRIMISLE from which there is no escape.

Religions are unknown on Shonak but are common on Earth. Most are based on the belief in a supreme being. In spite of the fact that many religions preach the concepts of love and peaceful behavior,

Earther history is rife with religious wars and purges and torture and executions of people for holding alternate religious views. The Earth of today is much less violent in this regard but there is still much sectarian violence on the planet, which you will enjoy watching, of course. To complete your education on Earther behavior before you watch any of the streaming or historical videos, we are presenting a number of bot diaries to you which give you examples of how they behave, in contrast of course, to how we behave. These diaries have been assembled by various Vid-Watch clubs to give you a representation of Earther behavior for your information and analysis and class discussion. You are all required to file reports on each of these which contain your impressions, your analysis, and any questions you have. Watch them carefully and record your thoughts for each on your student comms.

Diary Number One

Establishing Expectations - Introducing
Basic Earther Behavior Norms

Faculty Introduction. This diary provides examples of many common forms of Earther behavior assembled to show you how different their behavior is from our own. You will see and hear lying, stealing, cheating, physical abuse, gluttony, disease, deformity, ugliness, spitefulness, envy, and hatred, and combinations and permutations of them all. To be fair, there are also examples of love, kindness, and generosity. The following diary was chosen to show that people of every station in life are capable of misbehavior as a cultural norm. It is an example of what can be seen repeated everywhere on Earth on a daily basis. These behaviors are considered normal there but are totally abnormal for us and never seen on Shonak. This diary was compiled from hundreds of static bots in place there and illuminates for you the nature and extent of our surveillance capability on Earth.

Diary. Luigi was proud of himself and could be seen parading around, impressing the women of his neighborhood. He knew he could sing better than anyone else in there and often sang, loudly, out in the street in front of his family's apartment or from their small balcony while doing his chores. He was good at all the famous tenor songs everyone knew by heart and he sang them with passion and in a loud, clear tone that resonated up and down the stone canyon of apartments in the Vomero section of Naples where he lived. He was also a decent painter and had even sold some of his small paintings of the Bay and Mt. Vesuvius, to the GIs who had flooded the city after the German surrender. He could also make pasta by hand and was proud of his pasta sauce, which his family said was as good as Mamma's – high praise indeed. He also considered himself a great lover, or at least he professed to be that, even though he lacked actual experience at the age of eighteen. He had been as far as the door of a whore house but did not have the courage to go in, thinking that at any moment his mother or his priest would see him coming or going. He hated the whole notion of self-abuse as his priest would call it but that was at least something he could do without public scrutiny and it did feel good and it did take the edge off.

His slightly malformed right foot, a birth defect, had kept him out of the Italian Army but that had not slowed him down. It was the year +1945 UAY and in Luigi's native city, Naples, Italy, his father was a fisherman. Luigi grew up working with his father at the little harbor Mergellina, at the foot of the Posillipo hill, where the fishermen docked their boats, brought in their catch, and sold their fish to the public. His father's fish stall was there on this northwest edge of the Bay of Naples, facing the Castel Del'Ovo and Mount Vesuvius. It was easy to see how the volcano loomed over everything, still smoking after its most recent eruption the year before. The story of Roman city of Pompeii disappearing under a mountain of ash nearly two thousand years earlier was on everyone's mind and they all looked at the volcano every day trying to assess its mood.

At home, Luigi's mother was a wonderful, loving,

excellent cook. She accepted the fact that they were poor but now with the war over and the Americans bringing CARE packages to them with the flour they need, and even fruit, life was looking up. The years of the war had been exciting at first but as the Allies made advances against the Germans and the Italians, it began to appear grimmer and more dangerous. When the Allied bombing started in and around Naples, they all knew it would not end well for them. Mussolini was captured by communist partisans in the north of Italy and brutally killed; his body strung up like a dead fish for people to throw rocks at and spit on. The Germans became their occupiers and not their allies, and the Americans slowly pushed them out until the German surrender on the 8th of May, 1945. Now in late August, his mother often complained that the American flour was not so good as the semolina they produced in Italy, but that was almost impossible to get these days, so the Americano flour was welcome. They were able to make their own wine from grapes and other fruits they got from the family farm up on the mountain above Amalfi. That was a blessing and there was also the black market although things there were so expensive. Luigi wanted to give his mother more than his father could provide and so he abandoned the fishing and struck out with his own ideas. Mamma Francesca was grossly overweight, had a bad heart, and suffered from diabetes. She also had a heart of gold and was Luigi's favorite person in the world. At the age of 18 Luigi felt he could conquer the world, except his world had been almost utterly destroyed by the War. First it was the crazy Mussolini who created a fascist state in Italy, and formed an alliance with that crazy German,

Hitler. His notion of recreating the Roman Empire by invading Ethiopia and Albania were fruitless failures that cost the country dearly. Then it was the world war, which they lost. Two years of constant allied bombing raids on Naples had reduced parts of the city to rubble. Nobody knew how many people were killed. Bodies were still being found in the rubble, along with unexploded bombs. Now the country was even poorer than before and flooded with allied soldiers, mostly Americans, who had moved in and taken over. True, they were helping Italy rebuild after the war which was good but aside from basics like flour and fruit and canned vegetables from America little of their efforts had trickled down to the Cavalloni family. At least the bombing and shooting had stopped, which was something.

To earn ready cash, Luigi worked part time for his uncle Antonio in the family bakery, and he worked hard. All bakers work hard. But Luigi wanted more. He dreamed of having his own restaurant, based on pizza and beer, both of which the American soldiers loved so much. The Americans were the only ones with money, and he was eager to take as much of that from them as he could. How he envied them, and hated them for all their cockiness and money and the way the girls all flocked to them and not Luigi and his Italian friends. The Americans came from a rich country, with exotic names like California and Arizona and Minnesota. The Italians all half-joked that the Americans were "overpaid, oversexed, and over here". While a light-hearted slogan there was still a lot of deep resentment towards the Americans and the local communist party fanned the flames of discontent wherever and whenever they could. Luigi was no communist but he did not like the Americans either and yearned with all his heart to get rich, quick, and lord it over his friends and neighbors, and even the Americans, and maybe then even go to America where the streets, people said, were paved with gold.

Luigi's uncle, Antonio, worried about everything, mostly about having enough flour for his bread, and was reluctant to branch out into making pizzas for the Americans and anyone in the neighborhood who actually had money to spend. Luigi chafed at that, fearing this opportunity would pass him by. He urged his uncle to go to the bank for a loan to start the business while the Yanks were still there in great numbers, but he was afraid of the process and kept putting it off. Luigi gave up and went to the bank for him but they wanted to deal with the property owner, not his nephew. The Americans were quick to say they would not be there forever – leaving it open ended as to when they would leave, and Luigi was desperate to get the pizza business going. So he turned to the black market, with a long and storied tradition in Naples. The Neapolitans, and indeed most Italians, lived by a code they called "arrangiarsi" or living by "arrangement" which was a social code that allowed mildly illegal behavior, like cheating on their taxes, or stealing electricity from a neighbor. There had always been considerable organized crime in Naples and many others also engaged in whatever they could do that made their lives and the lives of their families a little bit better.

He knew that the soldiers bought fish from his father and other fishermen and he knew that the fishermen held things back so their families and friends could have fish too, or the Americans would have bought all of it, every day. Just one of their aircraft carriers had three thousand hungry sailors, not to mention their battleships, cruisers and destroyers and all the rest, many of which were currently docked in the Bay so their crews could take shore leave. There was an endless stream of motor launches bringing the sailors ashore and taking them back to their ships. Sales stalls sprang up just outside the gate to Fleet Landing and Luigi was beside himself that he did not have a pizza stand at the main gate. There were also huge cargo and supply ships docked all over the port of Naples that brought all the CARE packages along with huge amounts of other foods, medicines, farming equipment, cement, trucks, autos and lumber, just about everything Italy needed to rebuild itself. As Luigi watched all this happening in his city, he did not see nation-building – he saw opportunity for himself and anyone with the nerve to go after some of the goods just sitting there at the docks. With a friend, he broke into one of the warehouses in the middle of the night as armed US Soldiers patrolled the area, but not very well. All it took was his friend's sister to stroll by and ask them for a cigarette for the entire shift of guards to congregate at the dockyard fence – leaving plenty of time for Luigi and his friend, Franco, to conduct a swift inventory of the warehouses. They would be happy to steal anything they could carry but this night they were more intent on determining what was there and how to get it and what to do with it. They saw that the building they had chosen, Magazzino Numero 42, was almost completely devoted to an endless number of pallets piled high with bags of cement. Heavy and hard to carry, this was like gold to Italy, where there was reconstruction and new construction going on everywhere. Repairing bomb damage from the American raids on German occupied Naples was the priority but there were also the needed repairs to the aging infrastructure of the ancient city, founded in -350 UAY by the Greeks. New buildings were going up too and it all required cement. They left Warehouse 42, keeping its contents in mind and entered number 41 and found a cornucopia of goods. Canned foods of all types, mostly military C-Rations that could not only feed the American troops but also the locals. There were spools of electrical wire, electrical hardware like light fixtures and wall sockets. There were pallets of nails and hammers, paint in large cans, boxes of paint brushes, and stacks of tarpaulins. They were so excited by all this! They figured they had time for one more building so went to Number 40 and found gas cans, oil cans, grease cans, car and truck tires, auto parts of many types, and row upon row of army motorcycles! Now this was a treasure, indeed.

They heard Franco's sister yelling to the American guards, which was her signal that the group was going back to their patrolling. She knew Luigi and Franco were still in the warehouses somewhere so she got the guard's attention by lifting her skirt and asked them in broken English to tell her if her legs were pretty. That needed no second request, the guards went back to her at the fence and demanded to see more so they could say for sure. Franco and Luigi used this opportunity to leave the docks, taking a few small items with them as they went. Nicolina was able to cool off the guards by telling them she would be back the next evening, same time and place, and maybe with some of her girlfriends, so they could continue their discussion of her legs and maybe her friend's legs too.

That night, Luigi, Franco and Nicolina made bold plans. They would continue to inventory the warehouses and then figure out how to get their hands on what was in there. Luigi reckoned it was safer and far easier to let them take things away in trucks and then steal the contents on the roads somewhere. Franco heatedly objected saying it would be too difficult to rob a truck on the move or even parked in broad daylight with Ami soldiers everywhere with guns. This gave Luigi pause. He had not thought it through very well but considered what Franco had said, "Good points," he thought.

The next night Nicolina took up her station at the fence and when the guards all convened our boys crawled under the fencing and continued their searches. Warehouse 39 was full of coffee in cans. Truly a gold mine. Warehouse 50, for some reason the next in the line, was devoted to uniforms and boots and blankets and coats and shirts and hats for the soldiers, possibly for shipment back to the States, not for use here. But also a gold mine. There were also helmets, bandoliers, canteens, little folding shovels, sleeping bags, tents, stoves, cooking utensils, knives, forks, spoons, and metal dishes for serving. One of these metal cookpots would make mamma so happy, thought Luigi! Warehouse 49 contained medical supplies and bandages and stretchers. Luigi concluded that much of these things would be going back to the States or to the Pacific, where the war was still going on. He made a mental note to move quickly on the military items.

Having seen enough for one night they left the port and walked back along the fence like two young men out for the evening. When they approached Nicolina they interrupted the goings-on, which by this time had her asking the troops innocently if her breasts were attractive! These guards were hooked, and looked ready to tear down the fence in order to get at her. Franco said, in his halting English, "Come along home, sister, if you please," in a stern voice, saying her mamma would be worried she was out so late. The guards were disappointed but did not want to get in trouble. Their commander had laid down the law about treating the locals with kindness and respect, and also about fraternization. So, they slowly dispersed back to their patrols. They were infantry soldiers waiting to either be sent home or to the Pacific and had little to do. They had been assigned to guard duty at the port, which was a let down from combat but clearly a lot safer. They felt above it, however, as it was boring compared to fighting the Germans in the Italian hills and not something they cared about doing very well. What was the problem? There was a fence, right? And the gates were all locked, right?

Luigi knew a local man just a little older than himself who was alleged to be part of an area crime family so he cultivated a friendship. He was able to learn fairly quickly that the man, Andrea Popullo, was a minor thief but had no connections with organized crime, even though he enjoyed people thinking that he did. Luigi took him into his confidence and asked him if he wanted to make some money doing some things which were completely illegal but pretty foolproof, and very profitable. He was happy to agree and both Franco and Luigi swore him to secrecy, and they briefed him on the contents of the warehouses they had inspected. Andrea said he had an uncle who ran a pharmacy and would be eager to buy medical supplies from them. They loved the idea and set out that night. Nicolina recruited a pretty friend to go with her to help chat up the guards and keep them busy while the three young men raided the medical supplies. Each of them brought two large cloth bags. They had been used for grain so they could hold a considerable amount and were reasonably clean. They managed to fill the bags with bandages, plasters, aspirin, sulfa, tooth brushes and toothpaste. They also took care to leave the warehouse neat and tidy in hopes that nothing would be missed. He doubted these Americans, fresh from combat, had little care or time for keeping strict control of the surplus goods in the warehouses at the docks. From his observation most of these people, both officers and other ranks were too busy enjoying themselves and their victory and the fact that they had survived to be bothered with administrative trivia.

The pharmacist was thrilled when he saw what the boys had brought them and he paid them well. The boys, in turn, were overjoyed at their success and determined to strike again the next night. The girls also enjoyed their evening, having earned some money for showing parts of their bodies and promising to be there the next night. The young thieves put their heads together and tried to figure out what to steal next. Whatever they took, they needed to ensure it was light enough to carry and would not make any noise banging around in their cloth bags. Over dinner at Mamma Franco's they winked and laughed a bit and Manna knew they were up to something but knew better than to inquire. After dinner they happened across an old chum from the neighborhood recently demobilized from the Italian army, who was depressed at his prospects in this new, post-war Italy. Without much enticement he agreed to join them and he also said he could provide his cousin's truck in the evenings as long as they replaced the gas they might use. This gave them the idea to steal some cans of gas and while they were at it they rolled away two dozen tires, "Quiet as a mouse." Andrea said. They also managed to steal a large quantity of spark plugs and cans of motor oil. This they sold the next day to one of Andrea's cousins, who was running a garage, repairing vehicles of all types. He needed the motor oil badly and he was happy to have the tires although they only fit Army trucks. He bought the oil and spark plugs and took the tires on consignment. With winter coming up he asked if they could find some warm clothing and that dictated the next night's haul. Blankets, wool shirts, pants, winter coats and lined mechanic's coveralls.

Profits were growing and in discussion with the girls they learned that the supply sergeant in charge of the warehouses was one of the girls' "regulars", chatting them up and making advances and offering money for sex. They had refused all these things so far but were sore tempted to capitalize on their good looks and in spite of being good Catholic girls they knew they had to choose, and soon, which path to take. Luigi managed to meet the supply sergeant the next night while the other two were busy raiding the warehouses and he hit it off with him right away. His name was David Lopito and while he came from New Jersey, his family was from Salerno, just down the coast. Luigi took him into town and showed him around, taking him to the back entrance of a whore house where he absented himself for half an hour. When they linked up again, Luigi took him to dinner and plied him with wine and lost no time in learning that he had no compunctions in selling him things which he could take away openly. The Army was desperate to rid itself of its surplus rather than use ships needed for the Pacific Theater. He was eager to help his "countrymen" in Italy. He said he had never been to Italy before but he felt right at home. There were formalities in making these sales but the accounting was loose, cash was preferred, and for a percentage, our sergeant would ensure Luigi and his partners were first in line for the sales. The only catch, for this to happen, was to be introduced to his friend's sister, Nicolina. He said he fancied her and not in that way, but in a romantic way. Maybe he would marry her and take her to the States! Just what Nicolina wanted but Luigi did not let on about that. In fact he said Nicolina was afraid to travel and not at all interested in America. This did not deter the sergeant who pursued a genuine romantic relationship with her in spite of the odds against any matrimonial success.

Meanwhile, Luigi's acquisitions of goods from the warehouses continued to grow, the US Army was happy, Sergeant Lopito was happy, and he was handsomely paid. This continued for six months until a young officer arrived to take over the surplus property sales. Rumor was he was fresh out of college, happy to be in Italy, but sorry he had been born one year too late to see any combat. Luigi took him under his wing and showed him around, mostly to keep him from inspecting the warehouses and taking over the accounting. He took him home to dinner and the Lieutenant was treated to warm Neapolitan hospitality. This arrangement lasted for two months but then the officer decided he had seen enough Roman ruins to last a lifetime, was growing fat from all the Italian dinners, and said he was going to get to work. Sergeant Lopito did his best to doctor the books but the officer was very bright and could see right away that either things were going missing, or were being sold for too little money, or were not on the books at all. On the first night of his formal audit, Luigi paid him a visit. It was late at night, the young officer was all alone in his warehouse office, and Luigi came in and shut the door. "Ciao, Dan, how are you doing?" Luigi asked.

Lieutenant Sparks looked up, looking to Luigi like he was worried, as Luigi entered his office without even knocking, and said, "Luigi, you shouldn't be here. What's up?" Luigi looked Dan straight in the eye and said in his not-so-good English, "You are what's up." And with no pause, launched into his complaint, "Here you are, baby face from States, come to my country, you and Germans completely fuck up Italy, and you want to know 'What's Up?' " "We happy now making Italian people happy with coffee and flour and gas and medicine and we not gonna stop." He reached into his pocket and took out a switchblade knife and snapped it open in the Lieutenant's face. Dan was completely taken aback but not stupid and realized that Luigi was here not to kill him but instead to protect his black market business, probably aided by the supply sergeant. He did not, however, like the way Luigi was looking at him with that knife and wanted to defuse the situation. As fresh-faced as he was, he understood that the next few minutes were vital to his living out the night. "You needn't worry, Luigi, I know what's going on and I don't care. The way I see it you're doing us a favor by finding markets for the surplus we are desperate to get rid of. If anything, I want to help, and I can ensure that everything you are doing is done legally so you no longer have to sneak around about it." Now it was Luigi's turn to be surprised. "You serious, Dan?" he said, and lowered his knife. "As a heart attack," Dan replied. Luigi asked, "So how do we make this happen?" and put the knife back in his pocket, pleased he did not have to use it. Dan relaxed and said there were some forms to fill out but what it amounted to was to make Luigi and his partners licensed distributors of US military surplus. It was their job to find customers, take the money, and arrange for delivery or pickup. Naples was one of two ports where the warehouses were suitable for this, Livorno being the other one. Everything from Rome and south would come to Naples, including all the stuff from Sicily and the southern boot. Luigi's eyes grew large and, while suspicious, asked Dan what he would gain by this. "I'll be succeeding at my job, which is to rid ourselves of this surplus as quickly an legally as possible. I am under a lot of pressure to do so and there are many large Italian firms bidding for this business, but I can give it to you, tonight, if you like."

Luigi did not hesitate, he stuck out his hand to shake Dan's hand, and Dan didn't hesitate either. He opened a drawer in his desk, took out handcuffs and in a blink of an eye had Luigi's wrist in one cuff, and jerked it hard to pull it over and attach the other part of the handcuffs to the radiator pipe he was standing next to, It all happened so fast. Dan backed away quickly, out of reach of Luigi, who raged like an angry bull, or rather, more like a fly caught in a bottle. He was thrashing around nearly breaking his wrist, yelling at Dan, calling him all manner of vile things in his best Neapolitan dialect. He retrieved his knife and opened it and threatened Dan, who was still out of reach, then he tried to use it to break the handcuffs, breaking the blade and cutting himself in the process. In the end he calmed down, exhausted, with a very sore wrist, bleeding and very scared. All he ever wanted was enough money to get started in the pizza business and things had just spun out of control. He stood panting and looking at the Lieutenant as if to say, "Now what?" Dan had been waiting till he calmed down and then picked up the handset of his field phone, and three big MPs came in a moment later. When the MP's arrived to take Luigi into custody Lieutenant Sparks said, "Sergeant Trask, let me introduce you to Luigi Cavalloni, one of the men who has been stealing from the taxpayers of the United States." He reached into his drawer and took out his pistol, which he buckled around his waist and then pulled something else out of the drawer. It was his Military Police brassard, which he fitted over his left shoulder and snapped around his arm. Luigi stared at him, dumbfounded. Then LT Sparks said, "Luigi, you will be surprised to learn that my men are at this moment rounding up your sister and her friend, and your two partners, Andrea and Franco. We are taking back everything you haven't sold yet and we have also notified the local police, who can have you when we are finished with you. We have also arrested Sergeant Lopito. You will all be held for trial in our military courts under the terms of Italy's surrender, before transfer to their system. Luigi stared, dumbfounded, and for once at a loss for words. The Lieutenant then looked at Trask and said, "Take him away."

Diary Number Two

Earther Social Injustice – Social Class Divisions

Faculty Introduction: In questions of social behavior it is impossible to escape the inevitable differences between Shonak and Earth. While we know that it is these very differences which make Earther-watching so interesting to us here on Shonak, it is important to recognize and remember, over a long lifetime of watching people on Earth, how fortunate we are to be so unlike them. On Shonak we are all of a single species, race, and gender, with no politics and no religion, and no money. Earth developed much differently, with many different races and two genders, many forms of politics, many forms of religion, and many forms of money and commerce. In almost every situation on Earth you watch you will notice how all of their different motivations blend together to determine how they act and react to the situations which confront them.

Class differences among people of like background creates significant amounts of tension in quite a number of countries on Earth. Chattel slavery, a form of ownership of one class or group of people by another, is an additional situation that causes significant social turmoil. There are many forms of slavery but the most common is simple ownership where the slave is the chattel property of the owner, is not recognized as having any human rights, and has no way to change their status other than through release by the owner, escape, or death. Other forms include bondage for a certain time to repay a debt or other forms of forced labor of one kind or another.

There are significant numbers of Vid-Watch clubs devoted to social injustice of every type, including slavery in all its forms, and their feeds and databases will be available to you as adults. We do not want to duplicate those efforts. What follows is a story that shows how one Earther confronted his issues with social class and slavery. Once again, this diary is compiled from the many hundreds of bots of all types which were in place to collect the information for later compilation by its Vid-Watch proponent.

Diary. Sean Patrick O'Reilly was born to a poor Irish Catholic family in Dublin, close to the River Liffey and not far from the recently built Liffey Bridge. Ireland was an island in political turmoil, Catholic against Protestant and Irish against English. By the year +1801 UAY Ireland had been declared a part of the United Kingdom of England, Scotland, and Ireland by both the British Parliament and the Irish Parliament, both of which were firmly under English control. English landowners controlled much of the land while English businessmen and English clergy were all dominant in their spheres. The Catholic Church had found refuge in Ireland and held the Irish firmly in its grasp which did not endear either it or the Irish to the dominant and mostly Protestant English. For the O'Reillys, and other poor people in Ireland, politics mattered little. Food on the table, a warm, dry home, and money coming in were what they fought for. Their low, working-class poor station in life meant they were condemned to work hard, support their church, raise their families, and die young,   John O'Reilly, Sean's father, was every bit a man of his class and he did his best to follow the role set by his own father. Work hard, drink hard, keep his family in line, enjoy his evenings with liquor and cards and talk and maybe some fist fights. John was a violent, mean-spirited man, more so when drunk, which was all too often, and since his father had been the same, he considered himself on the right track. His wife Martha had hopes that John's skills as a marine carpenter would provide well for the family, and it did. What she had not counted on was his drunkenness and his cruelty. But as a good Catholic she did what she could to keep a good home for her children in spite of the John's cruelty.

Their home was small, very modest, but Martha kept it clean for them. She took in sewing for the wealthy women in town, who lived in grand houses, and she often wondered while sewing their clothes why she was poor and they were rich. What had they done right that she had not? Why, she mused to her few friends, did they occupy the bottom of society while these "fine ladies" occupied the top? Was this God's will? How could it be? It never ceased to amaze her how people of her own class reacted to their presence. When they entered the room, everyone of them stopped talking, as if waiting for some pearl of wisdom handed down from God Almighty! They moved out of their way on the sidewalks or the street to let them pass without altering a single step of their own. They bowed and said "Good, day, M'Lady" when they passed these grandly dressed women. These "ladies" never even paid them the slightest notice, until they wanted something from them. With the men it was often even worse. It was always, "Yes, Sir," or "No, Sir," and "What can we do for you Sir?" A gentlemen only had to mention to a constable that a man of the lowest class had done or said something they did not like, or accuse them of something, and their word was never questioned, no matter how outlandish. Why was that? And even in their Church, where they were all God's children, it was the same. The Priests acted one way towards the higher classes and another to the lower. Martha could not read but he had heard people talking about how things were in other countries and it seemed to be the same, although maybe not in America. John made good money but he spent the bulk of it for drink and gambling. So Martha was always looking for more work for her and Sean and the children to earn enough to try to lift themselves up from the grind of poverty and their low social station, since to her it appeared that the only real way out of being at the bottom was to buy their way out. She kept her eye on that prize even though she knew of no one who had ever achieved it.

Her husband never wanted to talk about such things. His life was complete. He had a warm home, food on the table, a family to do his bidding, a wife to cook and clean for him, and who even earned a little extra money so he could drink even more. Once a week, Martha often said to her neighbor, he was a good, decent man for about two hours. He calmly shepherded his wife and four children to Church on Sundays and acted every inch the devoted husband and father, but this fooled no one. He would confess his sins, receive absolution, and head straight to his favorite public house, returning some time later, sometimes much later, to perform nightly shouting insults at her and the children, most often accompanied by beating one or more of them on some slight provocation. True, he was a boatwright and made a good living with his hands and hard work, and he was valued for the repairs he could and did make on many a cargo scows plying the Liffey. His major failings were alcohol and a short temper. Everyone knew not to cross John O'Reilly lest he set on you with shouts and threats and sometime even his fists. The local constabulary knew him as well as the local priest – and he was often in their company after some transgression or another. His wife and children were the most frequent targets of his violent outbursts. He was always quick with verbal abuse. This or that was not to his liking and he would threaten wife and children with a beating. Often he would punch his wife, Martha, or twist her arm or pull her hair or kick her in the shins for little or no reason when the drink was upon him. No matter what she dared say or do to make him happy it was clear he just wanted to beat one or more of them.

Sean grew up amidst all this and in talking to his friends he learned that not all men were drunk all the time, or violent, and he nursed a hatred for his father. He also learned that he was at the bottom rung of the social classes in Ireland. Poor, uneducated, poorly dressed people were scorned and treated badly. People on the street scolded them for no reason, telling them to get out of their way, take a bath, behave themselves, "don't touch that," or "Don't steal nuthin," or "Fetch me that bucket," whatever they wanted whenever they wanted it. He and his brother and two sisters were not happy and always fearful. Sean was determined to do better. He secretly visited the local priest who taught him to read. Sean had said he was thinking about going into the priesthood someday which motivated the priest to help him. Otherwise, Sean was sure, the priest would have shooed him away, thinking he was aspiring above his class.

When Sean was fifteen he protected his mother during one of his father's tirades and was severely beaten by his father. He swore he would learn to defend himself with more than just reading and swore he would never be beaten again, and neither would the family. He was working for a carpenter at the time and was muscular enough but he lacked the skills to defend himself or his mother against his giant of a father. The carpentry shop where he worked was next to a place where pugilists trained and he asked if he could learn to be a sparring partner there, without pay, as long as he could learn how to box. The gym owner was happy to oblige and within six months Sean felt ready to act. The next time his father flew into one of his blind rages and began to beat his mother Sean stepped in and began to beat on is father. It was a fight they would remember in the area for a generation, and it ended, after nearly half an hour, with John lying dead in the street and Sean nearly unconscious. Of course the constables arrived in time to catch the end of it and bundled Sean off to jail while they sorted it out. Martha and the rest of her children were attended by the local doctor and comforted by the ladies of the neighborhood. Everyone knew that this was a predictable result and no one was sad that John was dead. The area Magistrate felt the need to make an example of Sean's handling of the matter. It was not so much that he killed his father, but the fact that he did it publicly meant that an example had to be made. The magistrate was familiar with Sean's situation and privately sympathized with him, even though he was guilty of killing his Father. He knew Sean personally from some cabinet work he had done in his home and liked the boy. Hard worker, polite, good craftsman. He was just protecting his family from a drunk , violent bully. He determined to go as softly as he could with the sentence while avoiding any apparent leniency. Since the Magistrate knew a man in the state government in Georgia, in America, he sentenced him to five years indentured servitude to this man. So, in March of +1831 UAY the bailiffs placed Sean on a ship bound for Savannah, Georgia. They took off his shackles on the deck of the ship and handed him a sealed letter from the court addressed to one James Mulberry, Esquire, of Milledgeville, Georgia, the state capital at that time. Our Magistrate knew Sean would be coming home to look after his Ma, and this would make it easier on him than if he sent him to "transportation" Australia. Martha and the three other children moved to her sister's farm south of Dublin to live and work there until Sean's return.

Sean's voyage to Georgia was uneventful and he made himself useful doing carpentry work on the ship. When they arrived three weeks later the Mate and the carpenter were sorry to see him go but Sean, who suffered from sea sickness, was not sorry to leave. He liked the people but did not like sailing! He reckoned he would do carpentry in Georgia and would look for transport to Milledgeville to begin his life there. After leaving the ship he was able to hop aboard a wagon bound for the capital. It was a two-day journey and as he had no money, he could not buy any food at the various way stations they stopped at to feed and water the horses. He managed to pilfer some grain from the horses and beg some bread and water which kept him from starving but he was constantly hungry. People looked at him as if he were some sort of animal and he thought that Georgia was just like Ireland in their treatment of people down on their luck! He arrived in Milledgeville late at night and thanked the wagon master, bidding him a pleasant night. He slept in a meadow, still cold at night in March, wrapped in his blanket, the only possession he had other than his clothes. In the morning he set off trying to find James Mulberry and give him the Magistrate's Letter of Indenture. After asking around and suffering the disdain of people he had asked for directions he finally arrived at the Mulberry home. He knocked on the door and a servant answered it. This was the first African he had ever seen! Up close anyway. There had been a few at the docks but not anywhere near him and he did not pay that much attention as he had his own problems finding transport and maybe something to eat and drink. The African woman looked him up and down and asked his business, showing some scorn at his manner of dress and filthy state. He told her he had come to see Mr. James Mulberry. The woman told him that the master of the house, Mr. James, had recently died of "the fever" and Sean hesitated in giving over the Magistrate's letter. The lady of the house then came to the door, and while cordial, she was also clearly looking down on him. She asked why he was there to see him and he said he had just arrived from Ireland where an old friend of James simply wanted be remembered to him. "No point in that now," he said, and bid them good day.

As he was apparently unexpected and unknown there he decided to wait to see which way the wind was blowing before handing over his indenture papers to people he did not know. He thought about going back to the house to ask for some food and drink but decided against it, and kept walking. Hungry, he set off to find any local carpenter to inquire about work. He passed a man carrying some rough boards and got his attention. Sean asked him where the lumber was from and he was told about the lumber yard. He thought the man was glad of the opportunity to put the wood down for a moment and the stranger told him that it was on the Oconee River, for its fast current, to power the saws. Sean thanked him and said he hoped he did not have to carry the wood very far. "Far enough," the man said, "But no way 'round it." Sean turned towards the street leading downward, towards the river, and it was easy to spot once he was close. It was as noted right on the river, and the sound of a big sawmill blade cutting through logs was evident. There were hand saws going up and down, and other tools making noise, and always the fresh, telltale smell of fresh-cut wood and sawdust. Sean reckoned he was in the right place. The stranger had told Sean the owner was a good man, "ask for Angus", he had said. Sean thought that this man was much nicer to him than he would have been in Ireland. Back home, he said to no one in particular, a man in his situation, carrying a bundle of lumber, would have cursed at him and kept walking, too busy to deal with the likes of him. Everyone back home looked at his clothes and dirty hands and treated him like some sort of sickness. He smiled and said out loud, to no one in particular, that he might like America!

Sean found the mill office soon enough and introduced himself to a big man with red hair and a long apron, and a ready smile. Sean apologized for his appearance and said he was fresh off a horse cart late last night coming from Savannah. He added that he was just in from Ireland and was a trained carpenter and cabinet maker from Dublin and was looking for work. The man smiled and said this was his mill, and said he was hiring good men with the right skills. He told Sean, "You look healthy enough, tell me something about yourself." Sean introduced himself as Sean O'Malley, changing his name out of caution, and Angus asked him some questions about where he was from and what his experience with wood and tools and design were and decided Sean's cabinet making was what he needed the most right then. He hired him on the spot for decent wages with the promise of more once he proved himself. Sean explained he had no place to stay and no money so it was agreed that he could bunk in the attic above the office until he was able to pay for lodgings in town. Angus MacTavish gave him a silver dollar against wages and told him were there was a public house he could breakfast at. "See the town for the day, rest up, take a bath and wash out his shirt, and start work tomorrow morning." He was told he would be doing cabinetry in the new government offices in the center of town. He would find tools in the shop in the other room. Angus handed him a slip of paper with the name of the man he was to meet there to learn what needed doing. He would be responsible for design and fabrication of all their interior woodwork. Sean blinked – such a huge responsibility so soon! He was pleased and a little scared.

Sean found the recommended public house and had what he thought was the finest breakfast of his entire life. No, he said to no one in particular, "This is my finest meal, ever!" The other patrons looked at him, and a little girl giggled, and Sean remembered where he was and blushed. When he had checked the prices on the blackboard at the door he determined that he could afford a meal they called "The Starter". It consisted of something called "flapjacks" with butter and sweet syrup all over them – he had never had anything so good and told the woman serving him as much. To his astonishment there were also two eggs, fried so the yolk was still runny, that came alongside corn bread with butter and honey. A glass of cool, fresh milk was included to wash it all down. How he wished his family were with him to experience this bounty! He felt guilty thinking of them as he drank his milk, into which he had surreptitiously spooned a good amount of sugar from the bowl on the table. He left there with a very full belly, and was happy to have some change left in his pocket, too. He continued to feel guilty that he was eating like a king while his Ma and brother and two sisters were likely near to starving on Ma's sister's farm back in Ireland. But he determined to send money home as soon as he could and that made him feel better. After leaving the public house he wandered around town, unused to the heat and humidity and bugs, but glad to be off the ship and glad he had found employment so quickly, and a place to stay out of the bugs and weather.

He sat on a bench in a park in town and promptly fell asleep. Not ten minutes later he was rudely awakened by a young man who stole his hat! He woke immediately and made chase, but did not catch the boy before he disappeared. He liked that hat! There was a uniformed constable taking notice of the chase and he motioned for Sean to come talk to him. He wanted to know who he was since the constable had not seen him before, and Sean remembered he had changed his name to O'Malley and used it again, feeling strange about it. Sean explained his circumstances and was quick to mention that he was employed at the saw mill by Angus MacTavish. He knew from long experience that the law treated the unemployed much differently than a working man. He said his hat had been stolen while he dozed on the bench and the constable laughed. He said it could be much worse, he could have been hit with an ax handle first but was sympathetic. He advised Sean to avoid sleeping in the open like that and walked away, continuing his beat. Sean shook his head and thought he might as well go back to the mill where he could gather some tools and get some rest or even begin some project. All the way back to the mill he repeated his name to himself, "O'Malley, O'Malley, O'Malley," he thought, easy enough to remember since it was his mother's maiden name. The mill owner greeted him on his return and asked him where his lovely hat was. Sean told him the story and shook his head from side to side in commiseration. Not in town a full day yet and already that happened. Nothing he could do but shake his head but then he told Sean more details about his cabinet assignment. The new courthouse under construction was to have bookshelves in almost every office. Also, the district judge needed an elevated desk in the courtroom from which to preside over trials and there were chairs to make, at least fifty, and benches for the public to watch the proceedings. They also wanted wood paneling in some of the offices and the courtroom. The mill owner said he had men to do much of the labor felling the trees and getting timber from forest to mill, and in getting lumber produced from the timber, but few trained carpenters to take the timber and make it into things. And he had no cabinet makers save for himself. They had a drying shed for the cut wood and used the oldest wood in there first, then the newer wood when the older, drier wood was used up. He was told to use the oak and walnut for his interior work, and the drier the better. That wood was in the smaller red drying building, away from the Georgia pine, the most common wood in the mill. Angus said there was so much building that using green wood was unavoidable, but it was no good for the finer woodwork since it would surely split as it dried. He added that some of the forestry was done by slaves on the plantations where the trees were felled but that he had none himself.

At the mention of slaves Sean stiffened. He knew there were slaves in America, and he had seen black men and women since he arrived but he had never thought they might be slaves until just now. It made his skin crawl to think that one human being could own another! Angus could see that something troubled Sean and guessed what it was. "You've never seen a slave, have you?" Angus said. "No, I have not, at least not that I know of." He was remembering the African woman who answered the door at the Mulberry home, and wondered if she was a slave. Sean said, and "I did not think of it until just now. We don't have slaves in Ireland."

Just then there was some shouting outside and the crack of a whip. They turned to look out the window into the street. There was a line of African men and women, tied together by a rope, being walked past the mill, up the middle of the street towards the town center. Angus explained that they were being taken to the slave market, this being Saturday, which is when it was held every week, rain or shine. Sean was dumbstruck. Angus told him a slave ship's load had arrived the previous week from Savannah, and these slaves had been put in pens to recover from their long journey on the ship, then sent to the markets. He said about ten to twenty in a hundred died on those ships and the rest were sickly right off the boat. They would toss the dead into the ocean and just hose down the people chained below from time to time, and slaves fed them, poorly, once every other day. Once ashore and recovered they were expected to fetch a good price at market. Then he said the Saturday Milledgeville auction would begin shortly. Angus asked Sean if he would like to go watch and in spite of himself, he said he would.

They stood on a raised walkway in front of a hardware store with a clear view of the auction, close enough to hear what was going on. The auction block itself was in the middle of a crossing of two town roads. It was made of stone, and raised about chest high, with a wooden roof on four pillars. Sean noted absently that the woodwork on that was nicely done, and mentioned it to Angus, who agreed, and said he was the one who built it, and smiled. The auction had started before they arrived, and he could hear the auctioneer singing the praises of the people being sold. Angus explained that there were two basic slave categories in this market, There were the fresh slaves, just off the ships, and these slaves were unproven, did not speak English, and were usually sickly in some form or fashion. They were auctioned last. Up first, and commanding the best prices, were slaves owned by local men. These slaves had records of behavior, could speak English, and brought the best prices. Then he motioned to Sean to listen. The auctioneer was hitting his stride. "Just lookee here," he shouted, holding a woman's chin up with his stick and grabbing a breast. "A real beauty and in perfect health. She will bear the owner plenty of chillin to increase the number of slaves year after year after year. Get her with a good buck and she will be whelping right along. Born in this country, she was, broken to the wheel," he said, and laughed. What is the starting bid on this fine specimen of Georgia out of Africa?" Men were shouting bids and the auctioneer kept up his curious banter, rapidly restating the latest bid and asking for higher, egging them on to keep marking her up. She finally sold for five hundred dollars – more money than Sean had ever seen! This was not an auction for the poor or the faint of heart. He told Angus the prices for slaves were higher than he had thought possible and Angus noted that it was cheap when weighed against the maybe thirty years of labor the slave would perform and they could always be sold again to raise cash when it was needed. Angus then added that buyers and sellers came from sometimes hundreds of miles away to trade here, "The finest slave market in Georgia, so it is," he said, but he could see Sean was upset by it. Angus shook his head and reminded him of the Gaelic prayer to God, to recognize what could be changed and what could not. Sean repeated it the way he heard it and his mouth went dry. He had often thought of it when watching his father abuse the family and had decided his father's situation was something he could change – and did. He remembered with satisfaction the final punch to his father's head, after which the light went out of those vicious eyes, and it was over. He clenched his right fist, still sore on cold mornings. Slavery, on the other hand, was a much bigger issue and while he might want to change it could see no way he could make that happen.

Then the newly arrived slaves were up for auction. First up was apparently a family, somehow still alive and together after their horrible ordeal on the ship. The auctioneer, always feeling the mood of the assembled buyers, sensed that he could get more money for these slaves separately and so he auctioned them off one at a time. The father, a tall, muscular man, fetched a good price from a distant buyer in the Carolinas. The woman only fetched half that amount to a local plantation. The two children were sold to different tobacco farmers. All of them were led off after the sale with much screaming and crying, never to see each other again. It tore Sean's heart out, or so he told Angus. He left the auction and went back to his loft room at the sawmill to process what he had just seen. These people in Georgia seemed nice enough but they had a blind spot on the issue of slavery. They sold people like they might sell cattle. "How can this be in the Year of Our Lord, 1832?" he moaned out loud? He was later to learn over and over again that the white people of Georgia, regardless of social station in life, i.e. rich or poor, educated or not, accomplished or not, were all "superior" to the African, who these people did not consider to be fully human. The Africans were also "godless heathens" and that further pushed them out of the human category in their collective consciousness, or so it seemed to Sean. Sean was downhearted and speechless. No different here than in Ireland, he said to no one in particular. Only the nouns are different. It was all about high-born or low-born, rich or poor, Protestant or Catholic, successful or failure. Here it was even simpler than that, but no less severe. In Georgia you were either white or black, and white was good and black was bad. In both countries the tacit understanding was that "God wills it thus!" He fell asleep that night with tears in his eyes, missing his family and asking, "What kind of God allows this suffering of so many at the hands of so few?"

The days passed and Sean worked hard at the mill, cutting special hardwoods for the detailed work in the courthouse. He was careful to match grains when joining pieces together, and prefabricating what he could in their cabinet shop. He made desks and bookcases and chairs and cupboards and whatever else was needed. Angus grew to like Sean and Sean liked Angus and everyone else he met but he did not ever return to the slave market. One day, when he knew Angus well enough, Sean asked him why he had no slaves. Angus paused and considered how Sean was against slavery and knew he was happy not to have slaves around.

Angus was also secretly against slavery but wanted to keep the good report of the men who did have slaves and who bought his lumber and cabinets. He lied when he told Sean it was not out of personal concerns for slaves – it was a community thing he was after and a business issue. First, he wanted to employ as many white men as he could so they could put food on their family tables. That was important to him since he well remembered Scotland, where there was not enough work for the people, and many were near starvation. It was why he left Scotland for America. And he was proud of the money he could send home. Then there was the issue, he said, of slave security. He would have to use some of his yard, crowded enough, to securely house his slaves to keep them from escaping, and he would have to feed them and give them medical attention when needed. He was not willing to do any of that. Better, he said, to let the slaves go do agriculture work so their owners made money which they could then use to buy his lumber and furniture and cabinets. As Angus walked back to his office from the cabinet shop, Sean realized that Angus was really also against slavery and that made him glad. He also knew Angus needed to keep this a secret and Sean would be well advised to do that, too, about his own feelings. This was The South, after all. So that was two secrets he needed to be careful of, in addition to his name change.

The years passed and Sean was made the master cabinet maker and Angus' business thrived as construction was going on everywhere in Georgia even as the winds blew cold on the political issues facing America. Sean still sent money to his family, but he really no longer considered Ireland his home. When he got a letter telling him his Ma had died, he wrote back to see if there was any interest in the family joining him in Georgia as an O'Malley, their Ma's maiden name. He had long ago burned the letter of indenture and did not intend to ever return. He never received an answer from his brother or sisters. In the year plus 1836 UAY, twenty-three year old Sean married Angus' sixteen year old daughter and settled himself with the idea of being a proper Georgian. Except for the fact that he refused to own or work with slaves. When Angus died in 1840 Sean took over the mill. He was almost immediately under pressure from local whites to take slaves in return for lumber and carpentry but he was careful to make it clear it was easier for him to operate without the extra care and feeding that came from slave ownership. One man was persistent and argued that he was going to sell a few slaves in order to build his new house and he might as well trade one for the massive amount of lumber that would be needed. Sean explained that he was committed to paying white men good wages so they could support their families and if he took slaves he would be putting them out of work. His work was not farm work, more suited to slaves, but skilled work he only trusted trained white men to do. That argument worked but to reinforce his stance as a true Georgian he had to say and do things over the years to convince people he was accepting of slavery. He was always ashamed of that but he feared for his family should they be tarred with the brush of a "darky lover". He managed to convince his fellow whites, but he never owned a slave. His wife, whom he loved dearly, asked him for a slave to help her keep the house. Instead of buying or bartering for a slave he gave employment to a local widow who needed the work after her husband died in an accident at the sawmill. In 1842 UAY they moved into a new, larger home, befitting a prosperous mill owner, and he continued the practice of hiring household staff from trusted mill families.

Five years after they moved into their new home, 1847 UAY, Sean was directly confronted with one of his greatest fears – being drawn into the slave issue. He was taking inventory at his most remote lumber yard when he heard a noise near the back fence. He heard movement among the stacks and bales and thought maybe a deer had somehow gotten in and was now trying to get out. He kept looking for what was making the noise then he heard the unmistakable whispering noise people make when trying to be quiet. He crept around a tarpaulin covering new-sawn boards and he saw them. There were six young slaves, boys and girls, and one adult, crouched down and looking at him with fear in their eyes. He simply stopped and stared. He felt they might harm him in their rush to escape so he backed up a good distance, keeping his eyes on them. They did not know yet he was alone so he used that to his advantage. He shouted over his shoulder, "It's OK boys, I'm almost finished. I'll meet you outside the gate."

The adult stood and addressed him in understandable but pidgin English. "Pahden, Massa, but weeze scaped and liketa not go back, not wanna die. Jus' we stay till it be dahk and then we gone. We not hurt nuthin nor steal nuthin. Food be nice if Massa willin' " Sean asked him where they thought they could go and not get caught and the man said, simply, "Up nawth, ain't got no slaves." Thinking they would never get out of Georgia, much less the South, he determined to help them. At last, here was a blow he could strike for freedom with, hopefully, no blowback on his company or his family. He said, "I hate slavery and I want to help you, but you will have to help me. I don't know where to take you that's safe." Their spokesman said they were headed up towards Atlanta where there was a barn church run by slaves on Sunday mornings where they could hide. He said, "They spose hide us, and feed us, and put us on the railroad for to go up nawth." Sean said he would take them there but they would have to promise to be absolutely quiet or they will all surely hang. They were amazed but trusted his word and when he brought his wagon around they all climbed in. He had the two older boys put lumber in the back of the wagon and arrange it around so they would have a space in the middle for the trip, covered in a tarp. They did as they were asked and he drove out of there, locked the gate, and drove at a normal pace in the direction of Atlanta. He had heard stories of a network of people who guided escaped slaves to various places where they could rest and hide out on their way out of the slave South. He trusted that the church they were looking for really existed and was the place to take them. It was a Sunday and there should be people there late this afternoon when he thought he would arrive. He did not know any of these people; the ones in his cart and the ones at the so-called barn church. He could only trust that God, and caution, would see them all through this safely. He reasoned that when he got to the barn that served as a church he could stop and pretend to ask for directions where he could deliver his lumber. That would give him some time to try to sort them out.

Probably just beginner's luck, he thought later, but it all went smoothly. He found the barn serving as a church just off the main road to Atlanta, stopped for directions, and took the slave acting as Pastor aside. He took a chance and told him of his real cargo. They were quickly unloaded and placed in the church hay loft – it really was a working barn – and none the wiser. They thanked him and he quickly departed back towards Milledgeville and home. As he drove away from the barn he felt a sense of relief. No whites had been on the road, he had passed none on the way, and there were none in sight ahead of him. He had done this good thing and had gotten away with it! He felt elation and relief. When he finally got home his wife remarked that he was very late coming back and thought he may have stopped at a public house for a drink. He said he did, and some super too, but that all was well now.

This episode played heavily on him. At many points along the way with those slaves he could have been discovered and that would be the end of his business and likely his life. He did not want to burden his wife or children with this, or any of his friends either, but he wanted to continue playing a role in the emancipation of slaves. It made him feel that good. For the next twenty years, until his death in 1863, during the War Between the States, he kept at it and counted more than four dozen escaped slaves among his successes during that time. In order to keep suspicion at bay he became an outwardly vocal hater of Africans and all things to do with them and refused to own any, claiming that they should be sent back to Africa where they came from. He said and did many things he was ashamed of, and never even confided in his family, lest something might slip and get them all killed or imprisoned, and at the very least shunned by all their white customers and friends.

While they pursued their busy lives the dark clouds of war were gathering. The book Uncle Tom's Cabin was published in +1852 UAY and it began a serious conversation in the states both north and south about the issue of slavery. The economy of the South was built on the foundation of this horrible institution and the white politicians in Southern statehouses and in Congress argued for their status quo, not talking about slavery, but about state's rights. All states should be able to decide for themselves whether they should be slave or free. Then in the Spring of 1861 the two sides went to war, with the slave states seceding from the Union. Sean O'Malley still thought of himself as Irish and had no desire to fight for slavery but the pressure to join up was immense. He held out until late in 1862 when he was asked by the Governor of Georgia to lead a regiment of volunteers and he could not say no. Major Sean O'Malley was killed in the summer of 1863 at Gettysburg. When he died he was not thinking about slavery or the South or the North for that matter. He was trying to do his duty and ensure his soldiers were not put at unnecessary risk. The artillery piece he was standing next to firing at the Union lines exploded, as they sometimes did, killing him and many of his soldiers instantly. It was months before word of his death reached his family, and they were devastated. They rallied, however, and kept the business going as long as they could, which is what he would have wanted.

In 1864, when the Union's General Sherman's army was laying waste to the land between Atlanta and Savannah, the O'Malley lumber mill and all their lumber yards were burned to the ground. Curiously, his home was spared. The officer commanding the men who destroyed that part of Milledgeville, Captain Middleton, had a job to do and made it his duty to burn the O'Malley home as well as their business. When he arrived there he found no whites, the family had long since fled, but what he found instead were more than a hundred slaves and former slaves living in the house and on the grounds and they formed a human chain in front of the advancing bluecoats. The captain rode forward and asked to speak with whoever was in charge. A large black man named Moses, with a thick gray beard and a bald head, came forward and faced the officer without fear. The captain asked Moses what he thought he was doing protecting the home of a rich white man. Moses very calmly asked the officer to dismount, and he said they had lemonade for the men if they were thirsty. The men were nervous by all this but dismounted and took the lemonade gratefully, then rested on the front lawn waiting for orders. Captain Middleton drank his lemonade thirstily, too, after watching Moses drink some first, and then Moses stepped forward to have a quiet word. Moses whispered something into the Captain's ear. The captain looked Moses in the eye for a time and Moses looked back calmly to ensure the message was taken seriously. Captain Middleton stood silent for a moment, then mounted up and directed four of his soldiers to stay back and protect the property while they moved to the next homes to continue their burning, looting, and destruction. The black man who spoke out, Elijah, had told the captain of Sean O'Malley's work on the "Railroad" and shared that he was himself a conductor under Stationmaster O'Malley.

The death of Major O'Malley left more than the family in shock. His employees and the "Railroaders" he had worked with were also sorry to hear of it and fearful for their futures. Sean's wife had sold the profitable mill and moved the family to Florida before the war came south, but she kept the house, hoping to live in it again after the war. She was well pleased when she moved back there after the South's surrender to find the home well kept, and to hear the story of his real feelings for his African friends. She had saved the money from the sale of the business and rebuilt the mill which was even more profitable with post-war reconstruction. Patrick O'Malley, Sean's son, ran the business, in the same manner as his father. Racial tensions continued after the war but the O'Malley family was a good friend to the newly freed slaves and a fair employer regardless of the color of any worker's skin. Martha hired back all their former employees, at least the few who remained in the area and were not killed during the war. She was a pioneer of hiring women and giving them more responsibility than just cleaning up after the mill workers. She also pioneered ways to use sawdust and wood chips for both domestic and industrial use. She bought numerous stands of forest and ensured that a tree or two were planted for every one her lumberjacks felled. She was mindful of what Sean used to say about having a sustainable business, from a seedling all the way to a dining room cupboard or a wood frame house. When she learned from some former slaves that her husband had been active in the transport of escaped slaves, hiding them in shipments of lumber and other building supplies, she was pleased and proud. She cried thinking of how much it would have hurt him to put on his anti-African act for the whites to see, keeping them from seeing the truth. She told her children that surely their father was in Heaven waiting for them and it was important they continue his kind-hearted actions towards all people, black or white. Unfortunately, her charitable feelings towards the Africans was not common among the majority of whites after the war.

Diary Number Three

Specific Historical Question – Who Named Alexander's Horse?

Faculty Introduction. Vid-Watch clubs often have questions that arise from watching their favorite subjects. They use the extensive Shonakian bot collection database to research and find the answers to their questions. They then share these with anyone who wants the answers or who just may be casually interested. Often, they come up with additional information of interest during these searches. This diary is compiled from the humbot's own thoughts, words, and deeds.

Diary. Humbot 307703.10.20.04: "This was a new assignment for which I was reformed and reprogrammed to give me the correct appearance and language and customs of my mission. I was sent by the Macedon Vid-Watch club because the Macedonian people of this era were becoming more interesting and they wanted additional coverage by humbots. Of particular interest were the political and military actions in the region which the Club could see growing more and more active and dramatic. The major actions had sufficient coverage, so I was assigned to cover the periphery of these events. The palace intrigues in the House of King Phillip of Macedon and his conquests were well covered but some in the Club wanted to see the ripple effect on local Earther lives by what was going on in this region. What was the common man doing in the midst of it all?"

"In Earther year -344 UAY I was introduced

to my village after seeming to wander in in as a newly orphaned eighteen-year-old. I was going to the house of Philippos, my "father". Philippos, another humbot, was well established there as the baker and I was sent to provide an additional set of eyes on target, and to help with his growing bakery. True, he was a tireless machine, but he could not do too much more than a real Earther without raising eyebrows and casting suspicion so I was sent to help. To explain my arrival Philippos had earlier admitted to having fathered me many years before on a trip to the distant village I was born in. He said he only found out about me recently, half a solar rotation earlier. My notional very ill mother had sent a message to him saying when she died, he should look after his son, Alketas. After the 'death' of my mother in that unnamed distant village I came to live with Philippos, the baker, in the small village of Sofitar, not far from the Vardar river."

"Being a baker puts a man in a vital role within his community. People want fresh bread every day and crowd their shops which means bakers and their shops are exposed to the gossip from the entire area. This provides entertainment but also alerts them to distant activities of interest, which helps the vid-watchers move surveillance assets to cover them more effectively. For the bread to be out of the oven at dawn to cool, bakers need to work through the afternoon and night. Breadmaking is a simple process but there is no way to speed it up. Bakers work very hard just to get the basic loaves out every morning. Fancy breads, pastries, pies and cakes are even more work and also in demand, but as bots we were there for information and video collection, not to grow a commercial business, so did not produce many sweets. This helped to maximize the infotainment collection which was our primary function. As a bot there was no issue about hard work or lack of sleep, although I complained about both often and to everyone in order to seem normally human, especially since I was young, new to the family, and to the rigors of baking. My story was that in my home village I worked as a day laborer doing odd jobs around the farms before my mother died and was not used to the regimented life of a baker."

"I developed a following of Shonakians who were interested in my interaction with the people of my village. I was diligent about inquiring after the health and happiness of our bread buyers and the information I gathered gave the Vid-Watch clubs tips on what sensors to watch for things of interest to them. Young and strong, it was my task to go to the miller every other day to fetch flour we needed. In my second summer at the bakery the daughter of the miller came of age and took an interest in me personally and became determined to develop a sexual and romantic relationship. Eventually she determined to marry me and began to scheme in favor of that. Humbot Control queried Eldest, Plus-Five Base for guidance since no pairing had yet been accomplished between humbot and Earther. If approved this would be a first and would lead to unknown results. The engineering of human bots was complete enough to allow for romantic and sexual function but of course the male bots were incapable of fathering a child with a biologic female. Infertility was not unknown among Earthers and the female usually bore the blame and the shame of not having children, but this was still new ground for Shonak and its fleet of human-appearing bots. The same issue held true for the female bots. While they could have sexual union, they could not bear children. What to do? The very perfection of the bot fleet opened the door for this situation and while it had been anticipated in theory it had not yet reached a point where a decision to proceed on this was necessary. There had always been ways to side-step away from it."

"This time, however, the decision was to proceed with the liaison if that was what developed. The Gold making the decision said it would play out step by step with a variety of decision points along the way. For example, at some point Alketas could meet with some tragic accident to either kill him or render him impotent. Same with the woman, Althea, who could meet with some tragic end. Or they could live together without offspring. I was therefore empowered to make the best of it and of course the viewing public on Shonak were extremely interested in how this might play out. Mostly due to the historic decision to go forward with a sexual union, the Vid-Watch club devoted to my every move had grown into one of the more popular up to that point. There was no sexual voyeurism involved since Shonakians are incapable of feelings like that, but it was certainly a scientific and manufacturing triumph to be able to make this additional step in the perfection of their Earth-human humbots. Of course, I continued to bake bread every day, but my personal time was taken up, now, with the developing relationship I was having with Althea. Naturally, I had no sex drive, not because I was of Shonakian manufacture, but because I was a machine, after all, with no genetic predisposition to the animal urges revolving around procreation. All I had to go on were vids of humans involved in such things and simply copied their moves as best I could. Later, Humbot Control thought it might have been a good idea to visit prostitutes to gain relevant experience for not only me but the entire fleet."

"Grudgingly, the village was supportive of the union. They were of the opinion that this baker's son out of an unknown, distant mother was an affable, hard-working man with good prospects. Althea was the miller's daughter and their union was seen as good for the long-term viability of the bakery and therefore for the village. The romance proceeded apace with me learning the art of wooing and casual flirtation and making her happy and dealing with the other young men of the village. One of these young men, Hippo, had earlier set his sights on Althea and he was not happy with her interest in me. He was a journeyman smith, learning the manipulation of metals for tools and cooking pots and utensils and farm implements and weapons. One day, some few days after the announcement of the betrothal between myself and Althea I was confronted by Hippo, carrying a heavy hammer and metal chain, swinging them around, outside the only tavern in the village square. I was in the tavern for some socializing/collecting before going to the bakery to begin the bread for the following day. He was calling me into the street to fight for the hand of Althea. As always Humbot Control was actively with me at the time to ensure I made the correct decisions to protect my identity as this confrontation played out. Control decided I should not surrender the girl to Hippo and walk away from the fight. That would not seem right, given the depth of the relationship at that point and the persona I had established as a mature individual capable of leading a family in this dangerous, tumultuous world. Of course, there was no danger of me losing any sort of fight with Hippo given my superior speed and strength, but I would not sustain normal injuries if Hippo landed a blow with his smith's hammer or heavy chain. It would not do the sort of damage to my body that an Earther would suffer. So, I was directed to meet Hippo in the square and try to talk Hippo out of the fight in a good-natured way. I therefore stepped out of the shade of the tavern's porch and said, in a loud, clear voice, "Hippo", "Put your toys away. Althea has chosen me and not you and she will only hate you if you hurt me. You have lost her. Give her up and go find another woman to wife."

"You bastard and son of a bastard", said Hippo. He looked at me with fire in his eyes. He continued, "I came here to kill you so Althea cannot have you, even if she doesn't want me – although I will soon see to that!" He continued with his challenge, "If she loves you, as she claims, she will give herself to me to save your life."

"Hippo." I said, "There is no way you will defeat me or even hurt me if we must fight for her today or any other. I was a wrestling and punching champion in my former village, and you are just a hot-headed boy with a big hammer." I continued with my own taunting, "The outcome of any fight today will surely result in your getting hurt or even dying, so best give it up and move to another village in search of a woman who has not yet made a choice." "Surely," I added, "A Smith can make a living anywhere, and attract a mate." "Even," I continued, "One as ugly as you are." This brought laughter from some of the men who were gathering to witness what would happen next. Humbot Control had given me complete freedom to pursue this and I determined to carry on as the personality I had developed since my arrival; smart, witty, good humored, but strong and afraid of nothing. I had more than once come back from the hunt with game meat or a wolf that had challenged me for the kill, and even a wild pig. With no witnesses I was always free to use my special bot powers. I could fly in search of game, half phase away in order to approach without notice, phase back in, kill the prey, and then do the same for any predator attempting to take it away from me. This was the young man Hippo was attempting to frighten away from Althea."

"Hippo paused at my display of bravado but since the village was gathered and more were gathering, he was committed. He continued to threaten me. "If you don't renounce her now," he yelled, "In front of her and her family and the village, I will have no choice but to force you to do it." He saw me pause than said, "Right now," in a threatening tone and with some enthusiasm, but we could all tell he was hesitating, trying to find a way out, but not seeing any. Like him, I paused, as if weighing my options, and then said, "Come here and let us settle this. But know this, if I defeat you in this fight, you must promise to leave the village today and never come back. At that challenge to his authority he let out a yell, and ran at me, dropping the chain and raising his smithy hammer as if to strike me with it. I sidestepped and let him rush past, with the hammer in full swing, and the weight of it carried him around and to the ground in a heap. He landed hard, got up quickly, and charged me again, this time without the hammer. Instead, he pulled a knife out of his belt and moved to slash me with it. Once again, I sidestepped his blade and hit him behind the ear as he went past me. I could have killed him easily but did not do so. He went down again and lay there a few seconds. He roused himself, got up slowly to a sitting position, and looked at me with hate in his eyes and in his clenched fists. He was breathing hard, he was in some pain, and a bit dizzy, and we could all see he was thinking about what to do next. This had not gone according to his plan. At all. You could see he was thinking: He was strong! He was the smith! He could crush me like a bug! He stared at me, then at everyone who had gathered to watch the fight. A few of the older men laughed at his discomfort, and he scowled even deeper. He stood up, a bit wobbly, and ran at me with his head down and his arms spread wide as if to gather me up in his smith-strong arms and crush the life from me. I sidestepped him again and stuck my leg out to trip him. As he went down, harder this time for all it was so unexpected, I hit him in the back of his neck and also his kidney, punch, punch, just like that. This time he did not move for some full minutes. People grew tired of waiting for the outcome and yelled for him to get up. He was popular, and grew up among them, and I was not a village native. They were all in favor of him winning the fight, but I judged they were ambivalent about the girl. "Get up and finish him!", more than one of them yelled. They did not look at me kindly and I wondered if any of them would come to his aid or even attack me but none of them moved to do either. After a long pause Hippo rose to his feet, slowly, and without looking at any of us, hobbled away to his hut by the forge. I stood my ground for a few moments while the people dispersed. I did not know if he would return with a sword or a spear or a bow so I kept a watch for that until everyone had gone back to their own affairs, then I walked to the bakery to start the bread for the next morning."

"That night, as I expected, Hippo came to the bakery while I was working on the loaves and he made to attack me with his hammer again. As there was no one there but us two I moved to him super-fast and hit him hard enough in the temple to kill him and he went down like a stone. I called my father from the other room and he called for the village elders to see what had happened. It was clear from how he was laid out on the ground in the bakery, with his hammer still in his fist, that I had defended myself, nothing more. I told them I had used the wooden hammer we kept in the bakery to pound large mounds of bread dough, and showed it to them. It was clear to them that he was too humiliated to let me live and he did not want to leave the village so he thought by killing me he could have all that he wanted. Humbot Control instructed me to act aggrieved and sorry for his death, I had meant only to keep him from killing me. The elders told the village in the morning that I had been wronged and foully attacked in the bakery and Hippo died in the attempt. He was taken away by his family and while there was grumbling amongst his friends the situation was all too clear and the matter was closed. I was told by Humbot Control that the fight was one of the most popular vid feeds of the P-Rot, which, from such a large planet of such violent people, was a very great honor for me. My Vid-Watch base grew even larger."

"Political and military events in the kingdom were momentous with King Phillip going to war against various tribes and other kings. Many men of all ages were joining the army to fight both locally and abroad, for the glory and for the booty, but I stayed in the bakery as instructed. When comments were made about me shirking my duty to fight for king and conquest, I asked them who would bake their bread? They grudgingly accepted that logic and they did like my bread. People even came from other villages to buy it, and we sent wagons with it throughout the countryside."

"A few moons after Hippo's death I married Althea and I began breaking ground as the first of Shonak's human-appearing bots to adopt a comprehensive lifestyle with a biological Earther female. She never discovered my secret life as a mechanical device and although the marriage remained childless, she seemed happy enough."

"It was in my fourth year as village baker that I brushed against local history on a scale higher than my modest remit as a small-village surveillance humbot. The king and his court, to include his son Alexander, were well covered by the many humbots and static bots assigned to the royal family. One day, however, as I was hauling flour from the mill to the bakery, I was attracted by some odd goings on just off the main road. Since I was alone and curious, I half-phased away from Plus-Five and flew to an altitude which would help me find the origins of the sounds I was hearing. I quickly spied a knot of people north of the road, in a natural corral of stone, with additional fencing, and groups of horses and men on foot admiring them. I reasoned that this was a horse auction and I moved closer to see and hear better to the advantage of my viewers on Shonak. In one corral there was a group of men in very fine dress and what looked like retainers, with one boy trying to capture a horse, or that's what it looked like, at first. From my vantage point above them I could just see them gathered as the low, dark clouds moved quickly across the sky. The bright sun shone through gaps in the clouds, so the scene was alternately light and dark, casting deep shadows one moment and none the next. As I lowered myself to the ground nearby, I phased back in. Now fully visible, a few of the men, all well-armed, took notice of me but paid me little attention. They could see by my dress that I was a local villager with no weapon so were not worried that I was there.

Their attention was fully focused on the action, which of course I was streaming back to Shonak. I slowly approached another knot of men, nearer to the horse being chased. It was a huge animal with black coat and very large head and bull-thick neck. All the men were well dressed and obviously of great means. I asked them what was going on. They explained that the young son of King Phillip, Alexander, was trying to break a famously angry, wild horse to his will. I watched for a time as Alexander circled the horse and I could see the horse threaten and charge him over and over again as he skipped away and continued to circle. Both of them seemed tireless. I was about to turn away since nothing seemed to be happening, when Alexander suddenly made his move. He had seen his chance to mount the horse from behind! Taking a running leap, and using a boulder for a lift, he jumped to the boulder and then to the horse, barely managing to stay on as the horse leapt up and away. The horse bucked repeatedly but Alexander held on with his arms around the horse's large neck and his legs squeezing its huge chest. He bit down on first one ear, then another and the horse let out a cry of pain and anger, bucked and twisted and Alexander refused to let go, either of the horse's neck or its ear! Within a moment the horse began to tire and calm down slowly, as Alexander beamed and cried out that he had won the heart of his horse for conquest! He declared that he had found a horse worthy of his own greatness. It only remained to give it a name. He glanced around waiting for a suggestion, apparently, and I said, "I had an ox once that was as mean and strong and angry as this horse, and just as big and stubborn-headed. Why not call him Bucephalus?" The boy looked at me dangerously, a mere stranger, but then brightened as he thought about it and said, "Bucephalus it is, then!" The men of his retinue asked him to dismount and they opened the gate to the corral. They said they wanted to take the horse back home for him as it was threatening rain and they wished to get to shelter. He announced he would remain on the horse until it was safely back home and fully comfortable with him on its back. He even said he would sleep on the horse if need be until this proud animal fully accepted him as his lord and master. In time, he said, they would become the best of friends. And with that, Alexander wheeled the horse around, pointed it toward the road, and galloped hard to make it home ahead of the rain. It was the first and last time I ever saw anyone from the royal family."

"My life in the village continued normally, giving the vid-watchers what they wanted to see – life in a typical village from this part of Plus-Five. Althea and I had a good life together. We took in an orphan girl which completed Althea's motherly needs and for myself, I made occasional trips to the bot maintenance facility to be aged from time to time, always while I was "out hunting" or "exploring". Althea loved the bakery and loved making her favorite breads and meat pies and filled in for me whenever I was gone for a day or two. As life progressed our daughter married into a local family of merchants and was well looked after. When Althea died, I told our daughter and the village I could no longer live there as her memory was too painful and so took my leave and they never saw me again. To be precise, they never saw me in that form again."

"I went to the maintenance facility, where my appearance was totally redone, and I walked back into the village a moon later as a young man again announcing that I was a trained baker looking for work. I explained that my home village, where I had been an apprentice baker, had been raided and destroyed, and I showed them the wounds on my arm and legs. I had big welts where the ropes had bound me as I was taken and held prisoner. I told them I had managed to untie the ropes and made my escape, not stopping until now, maybe half a moon later. I was hungry, I said, and exhausted. Then I told them of my second beating. While on the road I ran into some bandits who beat me and left me for dead, seeing I had no money. I recovered, slowly, I said, with the help of a merchant and his son who saw me lying next to the road. I convalesced with them for three days, thanked them for their help, then struck out on my own. Finally, I told them I had no idea where I was but could go no further. My name, I said, was Oppolitto."

"It was clear to them all I was tired and hungry and homeless, and they bid me welcome. With this kind reception I returned to work in my old bakery, content to do it all over again if it pleased Humbot Control.

Diary Number Four

Clarifying History – Cleopatra's Final Secrets

Faculty Introduction. Cleopatra VII was the last Greek Pharaoh of Egypt and one of the most famous Earthers in their history. The Vid-Watch club specializing in Egypt is one of the oldest and most influential on Shonak and was closely involved in monitoring every aspect of her life and those of the people she was close to. This story reveals an unknown secret to her final years and also represents the first-ever situation where a bot was required to give birth.

Diary. Cleopatra was startled by the sound of screams, and shouting, and people running. As she was raised in a competitive, political family, constantly jockeying for influence over their father, Ptolemy XII, the Greek King of Egypt, she was always alert to signs of impending trouble up to and including assassination. The undertone of panic in what she was hearing outside Caesar's villa in Rome's Horti Caesaris, got her attention and brought a frown of concern. She knew she was likely in the safest place in all of Rome, and as a visiting monarch, would have Roman guards to protect her always, so whatever was happening outside should not concern her, she mumbled to herself. She called for her slave Eiras, a humbot, to attend her and asked another maid to go find out what was going on. That maid never returned. Sometime later, while Cleopatra was waiting for answers, she was beginning to relax since she had heard no further commotion outside. She sent Eiras to fetch some wine and then four heavily armed soldiers entered her rooms, and the last thing she remembered in this life, with surprise in her own mind, is the soldier's face who swung the blade that took off her head.

Julius Caesar's wife, Calpurnia, came into the room immediately afterward, paid the soldiers a huge sum for their trouble and their silence, and spat on the body and head of Cleopatra. She then ordered the body quickly and quietly cut up into small pieces and burned in the villa's fire pits where they disposed of their trash. Calpurnia's slaves cleaned the chamber of Cleopatra's blood and clothing and other personal items. She had also wanted to kill Caesarion but now with Julius dead, he could be useful to her, his rightful mother.

This all began when Calpurnia, in shock after hearing of the assassination of Julius earlier in the day, had reacted out of jealousy and hatred for Cleopatra, who had the nerve to embarrass her by bringing her bastard son by Julius with her to Rome. And is staying in her house! Free from any fear of repercussion from the now dead Julius, she immediately ordered her loyal guards to kill the queen and dispose of the body. She may have wanted to kill little Caesarion, too, but Eiras had taken the baby to safety when her bot sensors and comms with Humbot Control told her what was going on. Eldest, Plus-Five Base was also informed, and he directed that the matter of Cleopatra's assassination be handled according to the wishes of the Eldest of the Vid-Watch club devoted to Egypt and the Ptolemies. That Eldest, a senior Gold and prior Grand Team Eldest, was unhappy at the death of Cleopatra and the loss of such a valuable source of highly popular infotainment vids. He did not allow the imagery of her beheading to be put on the public vids and he directed Bot Control to replace the Pharaoh immediately with a humbot replica.

This was controversial. Human female bots are far less common on Plus-Five than male bots because that hostile place is even more hostile to women. It is therefore more difficult for a woman to survive or live in peace and therefore more difficult for a mechanical human female humbot to remain undiscovered. This is because they are very likely to need to use their humbot powers to survive, and when this is done in public it can result in very damning evidence that the humbot is not human. In those days, before Earthers had advanced science themselves, evidence of bot-powers was attributed to "the gods", but Humbot Control takes great pains in protecting the existence and identity of its humbot assets. So because females in history on Plus-Five are at more risk, so are female humbots. For that reason, they are only fielded when specifically requested by some agency or other on Shonak, usually one of the Grand Teams, or the larger Vid-Watch clubs, as was the case here. They did determine that as a queen, this female humbot would not have the same safety and security concerns of women in common circumstances. Humbot Control, in an effort to put layered protections in place around her, also made plans to replace her key slaves and retainers with humbots. This would be achieved not by murder but by attrition and reassignment.

It took a full Planetary Rotation for the Cleopatra humbot to be constructed in perfect detail and to be programmed and put in place. By then Calpurnia had fled to her country estate along with her retainers and slaves and their villa in Rome was all but deserted. When the Senate sent guards to ensure the safety of their visiting queen, they found Cleopatra VII sitting with her brother, Ptolemy XIV, and Eiras and the baby, enjoying some fruit and drinks. While it was cool outside on this March afternoon, it was warm in the Villa with its heated floors. The Centurion commanding the guards posted his men at all the entrances and told them to remain until their replacements arrived. They were to allow no one to enter or depart. He took Cleopatra off to the side and whispered to her what had happened the day before. It was the first time she would officially know of the assassination of Julius but as a humbot she knew that and also most of the world's history up to that point. She reacted with shock and surprise and fear and concern all done at the same time and the Vid-Watch club was thrilled at her absolute perfection and how successful this would be, having a humbot replacing a Pharaoh! The Centurion, Gaius Antietus, also told Cleopatra it was the will of the Senate that she hastily depart Rome to avoid any threat to her person during the general period of shock and panic that was shaking the city.

The next days were full of events covered by dozens of bots and other sensors which need not be repeated here. Our focus is Cleopatra, and what she does in the aftermath of Julius' death. She immediately made plans for their return to Alexandria and within a week she and her entire retinue of slaves, relatives, retainers and guards were gone, having set sail for their return home. When Calpurnia heard that the queen was alive and well and returning to Egypt with her brother and Julius' bastard, she screamed and whipped the slave who brought her the news. When she was exhausted by that, and had time to think, and drink some good amount of wine, she assumed her guards had killed an impostor and had them executed. She then had those guards executed as well, to cut all links with the deed, regicide being a distinctly illegal act. She then left it there, determining that Cleopatra was gone from her life but she did worry about Julius' bastard son. She later worked diligently with Octavian's wife and with Octavian himself to ensure that the boy did not survive to claim any sort of family inheritance or to threaten to take over the empire.

Cleopatra's earlier than expected return voyage to Alexandria in the third week of March, on the Mare Nostrum, or Inland Sea as she was taught, was rough. Late winter weather made the seas and freezing rains, and winds exceptionally strong. Many on the royal barge, actually a specially outfitted trireme, got sick with the constant buffeting but Cleopatra was a tower of strength, tirelessly looking after everyone around her. No one could remember when she had been so compassionate towards others, especially the lowly among her retinue. It was also remarked that to their surprise, she did not display any of the symptoms of sea sicknesses she had shown on outbound trip to Rome. Their return journey took twenty-one days to complete, with several stops along the way for provisions and shelter and respite from the rocking and rolling of the ships. Her army escort vessels did not fare as well. One was lost with all hands and another was missing for days. The third was connected to her barge by a stout rope and held, keeping them close in case she needed them but also saving them from getting separated like the other two. The surviving troop vessel managed to limp into Alexandria a day after her own arrival. The captain expected to be executed but Cleopatra left word at the port to greet them favorably and feast their survival. People were heard to remark that the Queen must be in a good mood indeed, grateful for surviving a rough trip home safe, with her son and entourage. No one locally knew of the assassination of Julius Caesar in Rome that precipitated her early departure, but that news soon spread throughout the kingdom.

She was eager for news of things at home, and from Rome, at least that's what she told her advisors, but of course because she was linked in real time to Humbot Control, she knew exactly what was going on in Rome following the assassination. Her program informed her to be careful to avoid "knowing things" about these events before she was told by someone and of course, being a mechanical being, she was not at all frustrated by waiting. Outwardly, however, she was very agitated and demanded news every day, not only about Rome but also about her own kingdom as the news of the Assassination spread. What were the roman generals doing? They were scattered along the borders of the Republic with Legions at their disposal – what were they planning? What could Egypt do to help some and defend against others? Eventually Cleopatra was informed of the political crisis in Rome as the Senate fought to keep the government functioning while powerful families and their leaders jockeyed for power. Difficult times for Roman continuity at its core while nothing much changed along their distant borders.

At home, and in keeping with her character, Cleopatra determined that her son by Julius Caesar should rule with her as co-regent. Since Ptolemy XIV was in that role, he needed to be removed and she commed to bot control for ideas. Bot control was in uncharted territory with this. They were forbidden to kill an Earther, at least under most circumstances, ever since the edict by OE, but the Vid-Watch club endorsed the notion while also not getting directly involved. Eldest, Plus-Five intervened and offered a solution. Plant the idea in the mind of a trusted human advisor, provide money, and let matters take their course. So Cleopatra told her military chief that it was her wish to see Caesarion on the throne with her, some day, and then she gave him a large sum of money for his loyalty to her father and now to her. Half a Solar Rotation after returning from Rome in Ptolemy XIV was found poisoned and Caesarion became Ptolemy XV, Ptolemy Philopator Philometor Caesar. He was crowned by the Egyptian High Priest of Ptah at Memphis and lived with his mother in Alexandria.

The following year she was informed that a Triumvirate was being formed to rule Rome consisting of Octavian, Antonius, and Lepidus, representing the three most powerful factions in Rome. These three powerful men would replace the First Triumvirate which included Julius Caesar and with their five-year emergency authorities could run things without Senate's approval if they saw fit. Cleopatra was also informed that these three powerful figures were fighting each other for supreme control. Her Vid-Watch club on Shonak was enormously popular as the stage was set for action all over the Roman world as these men sought advantages through military victory and the death of rivals.

For his part, Marcus Antonius, or Mark Anthony, travelled to Egypt and Alexandria, seeking support from the powerful Ptolemies with their rich holdings in Egypt and the Aegean and Levant. He had no idea he would be dealing with a robotic replica of the famed Cleopatra VII, Pharaoh of Egypt, and understood that her sone by Julius Caesar was co-regent in name only, and too young to have any impact anyway. This famous pair of lovers met in the year minus 41 UAY. Their history has been extensively covered by Earther histories and fantasies and by bot databases and will not be repeated here. It should be mentioned that the three children she bore for Antony were a technical triumph of Shonak humbot construction and fielding.

This is how it was managed. Cleopatra-bot was perfectly capable of copulation with Mark Antony, but she always made sure he was either drunk or drugged beforehand so he would not be likely to notice any fine anatomical or emotional discrepancies. This was not difficult since he enjoyed his wine very much. Everyone expected that Cleopatra would soon be pregnant from this less than private liaison and so her close personal slaves and attendants were all eventually replaced by humbots. She explained that her guard chief (a humbot) had found an entire clan of Nubians to comprise her close personal guard. Large, muscular, fearsome looking and highly skilled with weapons and hand to hand combat they would be perfect in this role, and their appearance was indeed as fearsome as it was unique. They were all humbots, of course, and therefore invincible in their protection role.

As her pregnancies progressed the necessary figure changes for the ever larger mother-to-be were accomplished during nocturnal trips to the bot maintenance facility. It was easy for her to half-phase out of Plus-Five and anti-grav to the facility for alterations. She was close enough in Egypt that these visits took no more than a few hours. When she gave birth of course all the attendants would be bots but Bot Control did not want to risk making a perfect human newborn. The need for a replacement every week or two as it grew would open the door for mistakes and discovery. Instead, they saw to it that suitable women were given to be inseminated with Antony's sperm, recovered easily enough from Cleopatra and a few of his female slaves. Cleopatra's delivery was triggered by the delivery of these natural babies. When they were born the babies were flown to Alexandria and secreted into the birth room for Antony and other human retainers and family to see. The first to be born, in minus 40 UAY were twins, eventually named Alexander Helios and Cleopatra Selene. The second, in minus 36 UAY, was a boy named Ptolemy Philadelpus.

With their ability to phase in and out of Plus-Five's resonance, it was relatively easy to bring a baby from a distant place directly to where Cleopatra was allegedly giving birth. Those surrogate births were handled by a doctor and midwife who were humbots and also could help to ensure that the births were successful and the babies healthy. A second pregnancy was also arranged in case the first did not yield a live, healthy baby. In this way all three of her children by Marc Antony were born and presented to their father. The spares were never needed and remained with their mothers and all four women received very generous payments for their labors. This was a first for bot control and OE was immensely proud of his race for being able to achieve it. It was also a precedent which was used in later cases of a similar nature.

Affairs of the Roman Empire after Julius Caesar's assassination continued to dominate their lives as Octavian, Lepidus and Antony fought for control. Again, all that action is well covered by many other bot diaries of these famous people and their struggles to gain power. Our concern with this diary is the impact on Cleopatra-bot and her lover, Marc Anthony. And not surprisingly, the struggle to control the Roman Empire was a driving force in the marriage of Antony and Cleopatra. She of course continued to rule Egypt and her son, Caesarion, by then Ptolemy XV, was, at least for her, the image of consolidation with Rome, given his heritage as the son of Julius Caesar. Naturally, Octavian had a different opinion.

In September, -31 UAY, Octavian's navy defeated the joint forces of Antony and Cleopatra at sea and from then until their suicides the next year they were on the run from Octavian's forces. Antony committed suicide by falling on his sword after he was told that Cleopatra had killed herself. This rumor turned out to be false, but in the end both would die by their own hand. Like her, he did not want to face the wrath of Octavian and the blood lust of the Romans should he be captured and taken back to Rome to face them. The two had planned to commit suicide together and when Cleopatra learned of the death of Antony she too, took her own life. Of course, this was staged for the benefit of the priests and senior palace officials and Octavian's spies in attendance. She had summoned them all to give them guidance on the disposition of her children, her property and her kingdom. When she was ready, an asp was produced from a basket and placed on her bare breast. It bit her numerous times before being taken away and killed. The bot Cleopatra went through a convincing death routine and her loyal bot bodyguards surrounded her body in order that it be disposed of in accordance with her last wishes. Everyone was ushered out of the audience chamber and she was guarded until deep into the night when the bots all phased out and flew away. She had told everyone she wanted to be buried in secret with Marc Antony so their bodies could not be paraded in Rome as defeated vassals. Bots had earlier collected Antony's body "to take it to the Pharaoh" and his body was spirited away for burial in a secret underground chamber. Another body, a woman's body, of the same general appearance as Cleopatra, who had died of a fever, was procured and buried in the chamber with Anthony. Both had been prepared in the Egyptian manner of embalmment and mummification. Should archaeologists find them at some later date, there would be no telling she was not Pharaoh Cleopatra. Since none in the palace knew where the Nubians had taken them, and since they were nowhere to be found, Octavian's forces were never able to recover their bodies for public display and humiliation.

Octavian, who after vanquishing his rivals became

Caesar Augustus and the founder of the Roman Empire, was denied the final humiliation he wished to visit on them, dead or alive. He did have Caesarion killed, to remove the threat of Julius Caesar's son someday challenging him for the leadership of Rome. The three children of Antony and Cleopatra were paraded through Rome in golden chains to celebrate his victory over their parents and the annexation of Egypt and the rest of Ptolemaic lands. Egypt became a province of Rome and Cleopatra's children were given to his elder sister who had at one time been married to Marc Antony.

Diary Number Five

Witnessing Inventiveness - The Bow and Arrow

Faculty Introduction. Earther innovation follows the same pattern of action as Shonakian innovation. The first prototype of anything gives way to more efficient products and the manufacturing of these things improves along with the improvements in technique. The following example of Earther innovation will assist you in seeing how clever Earthers are. For them, as for us, enough dissatisfaction with something makes motivation to fix the problem.

Diary. Mugli was walking in the woods behind his brother. They were on a barely distinguishable game trail but not for large animals. They were constantly having to climb over or around bushes and under branches, but the signs of game looked promising, he had to admit. Both of them carried their spears, sharp-ended branches straight enough to be accurate and thick enough to not break when jabbing their prey. Carrying the spears made their tracking more difficult since they had to be threaded through the undergrowth they were slowly crouching and crawling through. At one point they were able to stand up, and Mugli was thankful for that, but as he stood up to follow his brother, smack, a branch hit him full in the face! His brother had pushed aside a branch and let go as he passed, and it hit Mugli squarely in his face, stinging his cheeks and eyes. He let out a harsh cry of surprise and pain and grabbed his face, blood flowing onto his hand.

Lingin, his brother, stopped and went to his brother's aid, finding that the branch had hit him with such force it gouged his cheek and made it bleed. His first thought was that whatever animal they were following was long gone now, given the noise they were making, then he thought of his brother and tended to his wound. It was not deep or serious, but it was bleeding, so he grabbed a tuft of grass and pressed it against the tear in Mugli's cheek to soak up the blood and stop it from flowing. He knew that it would stop bleeding if they kept pressure on it so he told Mugli to hold the grass against the cut as they headed back to their family camp. It was late spring, and the weather was warm enough so at least that was a plus. When the bleeding stopped, Lingin asked Mugli if he could continue back on his own, and he said he could, so they parted and Lingin continued to hunt. They needed the meat.

As Mugli made his way slowly back to camp he grew angrier at what had happened. Surely his brother knew the branch would snap back into his face! He may not have known how close behind him Mugli was but he should have thought to look back to see where he was before letting it go. He thought Lingin needed to learn a lesson from that and a plan hatched in his mind.

Mugli chose his spot well. It was a place on the path back to their camp that that Lingin must pass, between thorn bushes on one side and thick trees on the other, around an outcropping of boulders that meant Lingin could not go around. He took his chopping stone from his waist pouch and set to work. Stripping the bark from some of the trees he fashioned a rope. He then selected an appropriate branch and pulled it back, holding it in position with the makeshift rope. Then he waited. When his brother came back, carrying a rabbit he had killed in his hunt, Mugli waited and at the appropriate second he cut his rope and the branch swung and smashed his bother full in the face! Then he began to laugh, and laugh, and dance around his brother, who picked himself up, ran to his brother and they began to wrestle, Mugli laughing and Lingin hitting and biting him but soon he started to laugh too! His anger came more out of surprise than hatred and as he thought of the cleverness of his little brother he had to laugh, too.

They enjoyed the rabbit with their parents, tearing the little animal apart after it cooked over their fire. Their mother had gathered other food during the day as had their father and they considered this a good campsite. Mugli told the story over and over at the campfire and everyone remarked on it at various parts, stopping to laugh or ask questions. Father wanted to know what made him think of it and he said he was just trying to get back at Lingin for his thoughtlessness by teaching him a lesson. Father allowed that there might be some way to use that branch pulling to catch game but would have to think about it.

That night in the family hut, Mugli thought of his father's comment and fell asleep pondering it. By chance, a Shonak Vid-Watch club specializing in primitive cultures in this part of Plus-Five caught the family's conversation over dinner and immediately put more sensors in place to cover Mugli and his family.

The next day began another endless cycle of collecting enough food for the four of them. This was a daily requirement regardless of the weather or the temperature. It was harder to achieve in the winter with deep snow covering edible plants, and game all in hiding, but it was easier to track animals in the snow, which was the only plus. He also knew it was easier for him to be tracked, too. Now in summer life was less harsh but they still had to eat. Mugli was not very proficient with his spear, and when he did kill something it was usually after he beat the animal first, then stabbed it with the sharp end. His brother could actually throw his spear and kill something. He was envious, of course, and determined to practice until he was as good as Lingin.

Making more forays into the wood with his spear he time and again hated how the spear got caught on everything. Not all the time but enough to be very annoying. He wondered if a spear would be just as effective if it were smaller and he tried making and throwing shorter spears and he could see right away that shorter is easier for carrying but terrible for throwing. Might as well throw a stone as a short spear. And he did carry a skin of stones for this purpose, which his brother and father just laughed at. He remembered the branch hitting him in the face and his father's comment and agreed it would be good to make use of that effect but he did not see how to lure an animal into striking range and besides, a branch hitting a rabbit or deer would probably not kill it or even injure it. He was sitting in the sun, pondering, waiting to continue his foraging, when he idly took his spear and mimicked breaking it in half to make it easier to carry. He noted how it bent over his knee and then sprang back into shape. Like the branch which hit him in the face. If only he could make use of this!

He wedged his spear into some rocks and played with bending it back and letting it go. He did this over and over, resetting it into its rocky holder every time. At one point he bent the spear so far it broke, and he had to go and make another, which took him the rest of the day. He returned to the camp with nothing to show for his day other than some dry wood for the fire. His father and brother had done well so there was meat to eat, and mother had found some nuts and leafy greens to add to the meal. Mugli told his father and brother what he had learned during his day and said that his food for the day included something to think about, rather than just eat. His father said they can't live long on ideas alone, so figure out how to use this knowledge or turn his energies to gathering food. Mugli saw the undeniable wisdom in that and fell asleep thinking about how to use what he learned so he could put food in front of his family with it.

He repeated his experiment of the day before with his new spear and bent it over his knee over and over as he thought and thought. He was wondering how to tie the rope on one end and affix the other end to something and bend it and snap it back. He jammed it into its rocky holder again and pushed it away from him and let it go. It caught him in the forehead and hurt! He thought he needed a safety rope at the snappy end of the wood and thought he would then have rope at either end – what good would that do? In his mind's eye he pictured a stick with a rope at each end and wondered . . . .

In a flash, he was up and into the woods to strip tough, pliable green bark off a tree. He tied one end to his spear, just below the sharp point and the other end of his rope to the other end of the spear, The rope was too long and he shortened it until it was tight against the shaft of the spear, Then he took the spear in the middle with his left hand and the rope in his right and pulled. The rope simply slid down the shaft and the shaft did not bend, He then spent the afternoon experimenting with notches in the ends so the rope would not slide and eventually he was able achieve a controlled bend of the spear. The rope snapped against his wrist when he let it go and he began to think about how he might lure an animal into the gap between the spear shaft and the rope, and let the rope go and hit the animal! This just seemed too hard, then as he worked the bow over and over he gradually had the flash of brilliance needed for the next step. His "short spear" would finally come in handy. He took a straight branch and worked on it with his shaping stone until it was as long as his arm, thinner, pointed at one end. He fitted it into his bow and tried to launch his projectile but the rope kept slipping off the end of the short spear, He determined to start over with all he had learned, making the bow from scratch and the short spear and carefully cutting a piece of hide in the appropriate length before fitting it to the bow. He then took the short spear, now a proper arrow, without any feathers of course, and launched the arrow into the air. It sailed high into the forest sky, higher than the trees, and was lost in the branches, never to be seen again. He quickly made four more arrows and took them home with him with his bow. He ran into the camp, all excited, and showed his father what he had made. His father looked at the crude bow and arrow with pleasure, seeing almost immediately the potential this had. Mugli demonstrated it for the family, shooting arrows into a hide his mother had stretched on its drying frame. Three of the arrows bounced back from the tough skin but the last one, sharper than the others, managed to penetrate the hide. Father and brother danced up and down, seeing how this new thing Mugli made would make the hunt more successful.

For the next weeks all three of them worked on improving the design and construction, not the least of which was the bow string. Animal gut dried in the sun made the most useful string. They also fitted sharp pieces of flint to the tips of the arrows to provide more weight and more penetrating power. Lingin practiced every day and took his bow on the hunt. He was able to kill more game with this bow than he could with traps and his spear. They began to eat better and grew stronger and healthier. Life was better for them because of this amazing new hunting tool.

Late the following year the men of the family had managed many improvements on their bows and arrows. They used stretched and dried intestine from deer for their bow strings, twisted to enhance its strength. They learned what kind of wood to use for both the bow and arrows. They became adept at attaching small pieces of sharp flint to the arrows. Because they were difficult to make properly they hated to lose any of the arrows, either during practice or in the hunt. A stick with a piece of stone on the end was nearly invisible in the woods so they determined to add some color. White feathers were light and plentiful enough so they managed to put a strip of feather on the end of the arrow in the hopes they could see it better after shooting. They learned that too much feather slowed the arrow down and to little was invisible. So Mugli decided to split the back of the shaft with his sharp stone and put a feather in the crack, small bit sticking out on either side. Through trial and error he learned to accurately put small feathers onto their arrows to help keep them true to the target. Lingin, always the most athletic, became adept enough to kill a running rabbit with his arrows. They favored deer and also found the weapon to be effective in defense against wolves and bears and boars. If it didn't kill them always it at least made them fearful of people.

When a roving band of strangers came through their area in search of a better location to live in, they settled not far from Mugli and his family. First contact with them was friendly enough but naturally the strangers saw what in those days would be considered a wealthy family, living alone in the woods, and determined to kill them and move into their well-established camp. Mugli was sitting up by the embers of the dying fire when he heard their approach. He quickly alerted father and Lingin who came out with their bows. As the rovers charged, throwing their spears, they were met with a fusillade of arrows, well aimed and deadly. Six of them went down before they were close enough to use their clubs and Mugli, stepped back to allow his father and brother meet this charge while he continued to fire on the attackers. Shortly it was over. Father was down, moaning from a club strike to his ribs, Lingin was sitting on the ground, nursing his injured foot, and Mugli was still standing while the ten enemy were all down and not moving. Mother was in the hut in hiding and came out when the noise stopped, and went to father and Lingin to see to their hurts. Mugli checked on the attackers, slitting the throats of any still breathing. When that was done they sat there among the carnage, thankful they had their bows and arrows to defend themselves. Had that not been the case they would now all be dead. Father looked at Mugli and said he had saved all of them with his invention.

Unknown to them the youngest son of one of the attackers had witnessed the attack from the safety of a nearby tree. He had been told to climb the tree and keep quiet. He did that and now was there, terrified, and mourning the loss of his father, uncles, brothers, and cousins. Hours later, after the battleground had been cleaned up and the dead buried, Mugli and his family went to sleep, exhausted from the day's excitement and burying the bodies. Little Oog carefully came down out of his tree and quietly left the scene, trying to remember how his family had gotten there.   Long after dawn an exhausted child wandered back into his own camp to tell the women left behind how their men had all been killed. Thus the knowledge of the bow and arrow began to spread in that part of the forest.

The Vid-Watch club that assembled this diary queried other clubs with similar interests and were able to learn that many different groups have independently invented this and similar projectile weapons. Shonakians love technology and the people who developed it and this just made them more fond of these brutish, uneducated people, also capable of such inventiveness.

Diary Number Six

Witnessing Inventiveness, The Stirrup

Faculty Introduction. We have no horses on Shonak, so the idea of a stirrup never occurs to us but for the primitive Earthers, before machines for transport existed, the horse, a large, intelligent, trainable four-legged animal, was vitally important. The horse enabled people to move from place to place in search of better food and shelter, better places for them to live. They were also used by soldiers in combat, something as foreign to us as the taste of a pepperoni pizza.

The stirrup allowed people riding on the backs of horses to lift themselves up off the back of the horse, taking their weight on their legs, flexing their knees. This allowed them to rest their posteriors and also to stabilize themselves while the horse was walking or running. This enabled them to ride with less violent up and down movement but also let them use a bow or a lance or sword or later, a gun while riding. This made them much more formidable on the field of battle. Before the stirrup a rider on horseback needed to grip the horse with his legs which was not easy to do, especially if the horse was running, and the legs soon tired from the effort. Saddles helped make the horse a more comfortable ride, both for the horse and rider, but the stability issue was still a real one, as was simply staying on the beast. Once the stirrup was invented its utility was instantly understood but it was not so obvious a thing that its creation came quickly. The horse was domesticated and used thousands of S-Rots before the stirrup was thought of. Here is that story, and another example of the innovative minds of Earthers.

Diary. Tamarind was a young lad growing up in Anatolia in +125 UAY, and he learned to ride almost before he could walk. He was happiest when he was on the back of his pony and when he was older this was also true of being on his horse. He was a natural rider and good with the animals. His father raised and sold them and provided a good service for his community and a good life for his family. He sold horses used for farming and for hunting and of course for use on the field of battle. He did not care what the buyers wanted the horses for but he did his best to accommodate their needs. He liked making additional money by training horses for special tasks. Pulling a cart was a different life for a horse than carrying a bowman into battle. Trained horses caused fewer problems for their owners and demanded more money at point of purchase.

Tack, the leather equipment used with the stock, was also a good seller and Tamarind's two sisters worked with his cousins and uncles making saddles and braided whips and such. Tamarind often helped doing this. He did not like the smell of the leather as they peeled it from an animal, be it a cow or a horse or a deer but after scraping and curing it took on a wonderful smell he loved to inhale as he worked on various tack construction.

When he was eleven Tamarind saw his first real warriors on horseback. A minor warlord had brought them to his father's stables to help pick the horses he was buying and to help get them home. These were magnificent warriors. Their skin was browned and stiff from endless exposure to the sun and wind. Their clothes were dusty and loose-fitting. Their hair was long and braided or held back with a piece of leather. They all had wonderful weapons. Short recurved bows were made from horn and wood. Their arrows were long and straight and perfectly fletched, held in scabbards of leather tied to their saddles or on their backs. One of them, perhaps their leader, had a helmet with a horse's tail streaming from the top, and chain mail at the back of the neck. The rest of them wore felt hats and all of them wore scarves, which Tamarind knew was to pull up over their mouth and nose when the trail was dusty or in a dust storm. He was standing near his father when they rode up and the warlord dismounted. The warrior with the helmet also dismounted but the rest of them stayed in their saddles. His father had done business with this lord before and they greeted each other warmly, with smiles and laughter at some joke the lord told. Tamarind moved closer so he could hear and his father introduced him to the lord, who took him by both shoulders and kissed him on the forehead, then patted him on his back, and turned him around and inspected him like he would a horse or a sheep he was about to slaughter. He looked at Tamarind's father and said, "The boy is sound, like his father!" The lord motioned to his war chief, for such was he called, and, helmet hair streaming in the wind, he walked forward to also look at Tamarind closely. He made to punch him in the face and Tamarind easily moved to the side and away, grabbing for the knife in his belt. The war chief and warlord both laughed at that, nodding approval, and Tamarind's father beamed with pride.

His father and the warlord then got down to business, talking about what the lord wanted and what was available to meet his needs. The negotiations took several hours in the pavilion set up next to the corral in which Tamarind's mother and sister served chai and sweet cakes. From time to time one of the stable boys would bring round a horse and the lord and his father would discuss or argue over the price. His father touting the animal's strength, speed, and health while the lord complained about a perceived limp, an ugly color, poor gait, a bad tooth, and other such things designed to bring down the price. Three times the lord told his war chief to have a warrior mount and ride an animal. He pointed out certain negative things to his father who countered with other positive qualities. Tamarind, sitting near his father, knew that all these horses were in perfect health and condition, as did both men, he was sure, but the issue was not truth, rather the issue was price and all the various things that allowed the lord to bid less and his father to counter with more.

They also looked at the saddles and other leather goods the lord was after and these items were brought out by his cousins for their inspection. More haggling ensued. Tamarind noticed that his sister was nowhere to be seen. She has been hidden away from view so the lord and the men could not see her. Father had told him earlier that this was a good precaution because she was not yet ready to marry and when she was, she was expected to bring a high bride-price having never been touched by any man, whatever that meant, he thought.

As the sun sank in the west the deals were done, gold and other objects of value were passed to his father, and six horses and tack were taken in tow by the warriors. Then the unexpected happened. His father asked him to come forward and he held him close a moment, then looked him straight in the eye, and told him that he was to go with the lord as an apprentice warrior. He was to be with the lord for at least three summers and then brought back to him a man, skilled in the military arts. This would help him sell horses to lords in the future. His father held him close again for a second and his mother came forward to do the same. His sister was still not visible, and he knew he would not get the chance to say goodbye. He asked his mother quietly to do that for him. Then Tamarind walked over to the lord, bowed, and said he was ready.

It was the end of the summer season and fall came early that year. Tamarind was not used to sleeping on the ground with nothing but a blanket for warmth or comfort, but he was young and supple and soon grew accustomed to it. He was treated well by the band of warriors but as the junior boy in training was told his job was to fetch water and firewood and food from the cook fire when they had one. Their ride back to the lord's stronghold took a week during which time Tamarind learned everyone's names and a great deal about them personally. By the time they reached the stronghold he knew which of them snored the most, farted the most, rode the best, cared for their horses the most and which neglected theirs at least a little. He learned to play their little games and he learned to be obedient without question or risk a punch to the side of his head or a kick in his shins. During the trip they had done some target shooting with their bows and Tamarind used one for the first time. His left forearm still hurt from where the string had hit it and his fingertips were sore, too. But he learned that he had a talent for the weapon which the men greatly appreciated. He was not so skilled with the short lances they carried, but he was passably good with the sling. He thought this an odd weapon but soon learned that it could be effective at short range to distract an enemy while a warrior moved in for the kill with sword or dagger or lance. One of the men also carried a long-handled war hammer which he liked more than a sword but none of the other warriors carried one. They all had a few throwing knives which they liked to practice with, and he was fairly good at it, too. Longer knives used for cutting meat to eat were common and they were also used as weapons.

When they arrived Tamarind thought the lord's stronghold was not what he expected. He thought there would be a fortress of wood or stone but that was not the case. He saw a good number of huts made of wood frames covered with felt and oiled cloth. These were arranged in two concentric circles with an avenue down the middle so the warriors could ride in and disperse to their homes. The defensive nature of the design was obvious even to his inexperienced eye. The lord's home was in the middle of the circles as was the armory and the main corral for their horses and other livestock. They kept sheep and goats for the wool and for the milk. There were oxen to pull the carts lined up at the back of the corral. Tamarind could see that they could move the entire village fairly easily. He asked the war chief, Turuk, how often they moved, and he smiled, pleased that Tamarind saw so quickly that this is what they

did. He said, "When the game and the raiding and the
pasturing gives out, we move to less spoiled lands. There
is no set time for this – but we all know when we need to
relocate. We think that by this time next year we will be
in a different home, likely in the direction of the setting
sun. Our scouts have already found a suitable place and
next week we will go with our lord to see it. We could
actually move this year, as the freezing weather is still
far enough off but the lord will decide next week. Would
you like to go with us?" "It will be another seven to ten
more days sleeping on the ground." He considered it for
about four heartbeats then said, "Yes, I want to go with
you all." So that was settled and without even spending
one night at "home" they set out on their journey with
their lord to survey the proposed new settlement site.
The lord said he needed to see it immediately if they
were going to move this season. So off they went. It was
harder going since there were some mountains to cross
and rivers to find the fords for but they made it to the
site in just six days. Tamarind's sore buttocks reminded
him he was not used to so much time on horseback, even
with a supposedly comfortable saddle. He turned over
in him mind some improvements he could make in the
design. The lord spent a day exploring the surrounding
terrain and pronounced it worth moving to now, before
winter. He dispatched two of his warriors to return to
their camp in haste to tell everyone to begin the process
of moving. This was not a trivial thing to do as everything
they intended to use at their new home had to be
dismantled and prepared for shipment. If they did not
have sufficient carts they would have to drag or carry the
excess. It was possible to make two trips but it was late

in the season for such a plan, but they could do it, just, especially if the weather did not turn too cold too early. There would be snow in the mountains they crossed, hopefully not too deep just yet. Tamarind remained with the lord and his ten warriors, which included his war chief. Turuk was keen to find any evidence of people in the area so he sent his scouts in four directions to look for signs and report back if they found any. He told them not to try to find the people, just find their signs. Three days later the scouts who went south rode back to report that there were people in that direction but did not try to find out who they were or how many there were. When all the scouts returned he split his party in half, one half to guard this new site and the other to go south and find these people. None of the other scouts saw any signs of people so this was considered prudent by everyone. Tamarind was told to stay with the camp. The lord explained his skill with his bow was needed to defend it but he was thinking of Tamarind's father and how disappointed he would be if his son were killed on such a blind scouting trip as he was undertaking.

On the third night at the new camp they were all relaxed and going about their preparation for sleep when the first fusillade of arrows came sailing through. Two of the guards went down immediately and two more as they went for their own bows. Only Tamarind was left and he played dead as the bowmen came in the camp. They did not even look at him at first and then the lord and his party came bursting into the camp on their war horses and cut down the four marauders as they turned and ran. As usual in this time and place the actual fighting was short lived. The four marauders were killed almost immediately while the returning warriors continued into the woods looking for any others who may be lurking nearby. One such was cut down immediately and another was running swiftly away when one of their bowmen shot him down. No more were to be seen or heard but they kept watch all night from perches in the trees around the meadow they were to camp in. The lord was relieved to find Tamarind alive and unhurt but noted the arrow stuck in the saddle he had been resting on around the campfire. If they had not come on the scene when they did Tamarind would surely be dead now.

They first buried their own dead and mourned for them. They were loyal, true and good friends. They died a warrior's death with no thought of anything to detract from their honored lives. Then they slept for the night and in the morning they turned their attention to the enemy dead. When they had finished stripping them of anything useful they did not bury them but rather cut them into pieces and threw them into the nearby river. They kept their heads and placed them on poles at intervals around their camp. Then there was time for discussion and planning. The lord wanted to move here more than ever after seeing the rich plunder available to the south and from their clothing he concluded that these bandits were related to those people. Since they were only there a few days he thought these men were a hunting party who had simply happened on his camp and attacked it without much consideration. He was about to move a community of some six hundred people into their new homes here and his more than two hundred and fifty warriors would soon find lucrative raiding opportunities. He was hopeful that there had been no survivors from this recent raid to alert the locals of this new presence. They were extremely vulnerable in such a small party of six warriors and a boy. He talked it over with the war chief and they decided to decamp for the time being into the nearby hills where they could keep watch and wait for their people to arrive. This proved to be a wise move.

Two days after they relocated they saw from their hilltop perch a party of some fifty warriors, half on horseback. He had not seen such a force on their earlier reconnaissance and was surprised but not overly concerned. The warriors, led by a large man on a huge war horse, collected the heads left on poles and buried them without ceremony. Then they made camp and sent out patrols to find the trail of the lord's party. There had been a cold, hard rain the previous day and night and all traces of their movement had been obscured. The lord thanked the gods for that. Fearless, he was, but he was not stupid. There was no way he could hope to survive a pitched battle with such a force as was now looking for him. They were a group of seven people and eleven horses which did not take up much space but they did make noise and the horses especially were liable to react to the presence of the war party horses when they thought to look in his direction. He decided to move out quickly and quietly in the direction of their convoy. They did so immediately and kept going long after they considered it safe to slow down. Two days into their march they ran into the convoy's advance scouts and were relieved to see them. The lord was told that the main body was two days behind them, maybe three, and the rear guard another day behind them. The advance guard consisted of twenty warriors on horseback which did not give the lord sufficient numbers to fight the force behind them. The lord told them what their situation was and they began to fall back toward the main body of the convoy and the bulk of their cavalry. Their horses were exhausted, and they were not much better off so they rode only until sundown and made camp. They were on an open plain at that point so had confidence they could not be surprised by any force, but they kept a robust guard through the night.

The lord's party told the tail of the attack and their chase into the woods on horseback. One of the warriors, the one who had shot the last of the bandits with his bow, complained that riding through trees on a horse, something they were not accustomed to, was extremely difficult as the horse had to jerk left and right and left again to avoid trees and bushes and deadfall. The rider had to be wary of low branches and so it was all they could do to hang on much less fire a bow.

Tamarind heard this and immediately went to work with the spare leather from one of their dead warrior's kit. By morning, he fashioned a crude but strong prototype of his invention and asked them all to watch. He first threw his strap over the horse, under the saddle, and then put on the saddle. He explained that if he had his tools and leather kit he would attach his thing to the saddle but in the interim this would have to do. He asked for a toss up to the saddle which one of the warriors was happy to do and he then put his feet into the loops he fashioned in the straps. Then he did a remarkable thing. He stood up! The more intelligent warriors saw immediately how advantageous this was and shouted and applauded and all said they wanted to try it. Throughout the next day, as they rested, Tamarind and two other warriors figured out how to attach these loops to the saddles and also put a stout piece of wood in the loop to keep it open to accept the foot. Then they rode around learning how to adjust the length to each warrior's legs to allow sufficient room between their butts and the saddle when standing up. They were astonished at how much more stable they were and therefore how much better they could use a sword or a lance or a bow while galloping into battle. The most dangerous part of battle while on a horse is when they were caught in an infantry melee, spending half their concentration and energy just trying to stay on the horse. With these stirrups they need not enter the melee at all, but could ride around the rear and flanks of the enemy shooting them with accurately placed arrows. The lord was so pleased and proud of what his warriors could now accomplish he decided that their number was sufficient to defeat the fifty warriors on their trail. The next morning, he was forced to put his judgment to the test.

The party of warriors chasing our lord and his now twenty six warriors and a boy caught up to them and halted just out of bow shot. Our lord did not want to charge dismounted bowmen so waited for them to mount up and charge, which they did very quickly. He then ordered his forces to split into two groups of ten with a third group of six (including Tamarind) constituting a reserve in the rear. The enemy war chief was surprised to see them charging his own charge, but the die was cast and they thundered towards each other. Our lord's forces split far to the left and right to encircle the oncoming fifty which made them thin their own line as they spread out to keep from being flanked. But as these maneuvers were taking place, our lord's warriors began to stand up and fire their arrows with deadly accuracy. They all either hit a rider or a horse and then they reloaded and fired again while the enemy just kept riding. When our lord's force passed the enemy and turned to follow them, they turned to face them and the same thing happened again. The enemy tried to fumble with their own bows and ready their lances only to be cut down. By this time twenty of the enemy were dead or dying and another ten were on foot and scrambling to get their bows from their dead horse's saddle. They became the targets of the reserve who had ridden up to join the fight. They were all dropped quickly. The numbers were now even but dwindling fast in our lord's favor. He had lost only one horse and one warrior to lucky bow shots. The enemy chief went down along with his horse and the slaughter continued as our lord's riders kept circling the enemy firing accurately into their midst. In less than half an hour it was all over. Our lord lost another two warriors and another horse but all fifty of the enemy were dead. When it was over they simply sat on their mounts and stared at what they had done, and how well, all due to the advantage of the stirrup, made by the horse trader's kid! They thronged to him and carried him off his horse and onto their shoulder and slowly let the adrenalin leave them to calm themselves for the grisly task of dealing with the dead. First their own then the enemy. Once again they ceremoniously buried their dead and gave them the respect they deserved as warriors killed in battle. Their families would receive their share of the loot.

The enemy dead were not buried but were left for the crows and wolves, after everything of use was taken off them. The war chief had excellent weapons which our lord gave to his own war chief rather than claim any of it for himself. He did claim the nice fur shoulder piece the enemy chief was wearing and his boots which were of excellent construction. The rest of the men enjoyed the plunder of such a large group of enemy. The lord directed that all money found on the dead would be pooled and divided evenly according to their custom, which included the families of their dead warriors, and this proved a handsome bonus. He also directed that all his mounted warriors would be fitted out with the stirrup immediately, as they continued their relocation convoy. He sent a rider to the rear guard to show them their stirrups so they could begin to make them as well. That night, a league upwind from the battlefield, at their camp fire, and after eating, the lord asked Tamarind to come forward. He did so and the lord hugged him, slapped him on the back, and told him he was now a blooded warrior of his clan, having killed one horse and two of the enemy warriors. He also said he could have his pick of the clan daughters not already spoken for. Tamarind, just now twelve summers, thanked the chief but then stupidly asked the lord would he do with any of the daughters! This received gales of laughter from the men, who understood, and the lord said that if not now, then whenever he wanted to. Several fathers approached him with information about their daughters and invited him to join them at their new home when they were resettled. These warriors would be pleased and proud to have such a son in law. Tamarind thanked them all and he went to sleep that night among his friends and fellow warriors. As he drifted off he realized that his invention was simply borne of necessity, but his combination of riding experience, coupled with his experience with tack, and the emergency they faced, all mixed together in his mind and his hands got to work. He was not a genius but he was the right person in the right place at the right time to help his fellow warriors carry the day! He was smiling as he fell asleep.

In the morning, after eating cheese and salted goat, the lord and war chief and his more experienced warriors sat to discuss the experience of their victory the day before. They were sure that never before had such a victory been achieved but Turuk cautioned that while the stirrup was the game changer it was only so since the other force did not have it. And it was not the only reason they prevailed. They did not meet their enemy head on, which would have been a disaster. They split into three groups, two riding out to turn their flanks and a reserve which was there to handle the dismounted bowmen. So it was a combination of tactics and equipment which saw them to victory. But, he agreed, they needed to keep this new capability, the stirrup, a secret as long as possible, and they also needed to formulate tactics against a time when the other side would also have them. It would only take one witness to take back the news to cause a revolution in mounted warfare.

Diary Number Seven

Solving Mysteries – The Lost Colony of Roanoke

Faculty Introduction. This Diary shows that you can solve a "mystery" by piecing together a narrative for a situation that had only minimal bot coverage.

One of the most frustrating situations for any Vid-Watch club is the lack of source material. Shonak prides itself on its extensive infotainment surveillance coverage of Plus-Five/Earth. This has led to high expectations that precise answers can be found to even the most trivial questions. However, the situation surrounding what would be called The Lost Colony of Roanoke was only sparsely covered by Shonakian surveillance. This was an event taking place at a time and in a place where there was little interest on Shonak and consequently there had not been many requests for coverage. By unfortunate chance the ship the colonists used also had only modest surveillance coverage and this led to some significant gaps in collection. Further exacerbating the situation was the fact that there was no champion on Shonak for the coverage of these people as they were not a target for any clubs. What gap fillers there are exist only because there was some minimal interest in the natives on the continent and in the place where the colonists settled. And of course minimal interest meant minimal surveillance coverage, which makes this next diary so challenging – and Shonakians love a challenge.

Diary. Elizabeth I, Queen of England, wanted to secure land and riches from the new world like England's rival, Spain was doing. She encouraged the establishment of colonies in the New World to assist in gaining a foothold on this vast, uncharted continent.

The first English voyage, in +1584 UAY, was exploratory in nature designed to find suitable places from which to raid Spanish ships returning to Europe laden with gold and silver. During their six-week stay they mapped and explored and spent most of their time fifty miles south of Roanoke at Croatoan Island where they befriended the Croatan tribe. Two native men, Manteo and Wanchese were taken with them back to England to show everyone natives from the new world and to impress the Queen, and her advisors, that they had indeed been to the New World.

The second voyage consisted of seven ships and more than 600 men and lasted 11 months. Manteo and Wanchese returned home with this fleet. This was not a colonization force; this was a military action designed to raid Spanish ships calling along the coast for fresh water on their way back to Spain. One of the English ships ran aground and to make up for the loss, the leader of the expedition took all but 100 of the men and headed south to raid Spanish towns and shipping in the Caribbean. He told them he would return with supplies and they could continue their mission. The leader of the group of one hundred men left behind, Captain Lane, set up their fort at Roanoke Island and very soon went to war with some of the local native tribes. After ten months Lane and his men had run through their supplies and were near starvation. They spotted Sir Francis Drake's ships passing north and were able to secure passage home on their ships, blaming their leader for failure to return with supplies. This failed military venture set up the disastrous situation that would be faced in +1587 UAY by the colonists under Governor White.

In that year the second expedition to form a permanent colonial settlement set sail under the appointed governor, John White, with more than 100 men, women, and children. This group consisted of some twenty families and acquaintances all hoping to start new life and seek their fortunes in the New World. Their intended destination was Chesapeake Bay, where the harbors were deep and the natives friendly. Unfortunately for the people on this expedition, landfall was made at Roanoke, and the captain left them there instead of taking them north to Chesapeake. He deliberately allowed them all to disembark for dry land after the arduous journey but unexpectedly would not let them re-board. Governor White was furious but the crew were under instructions to allow none to re board their ship, the Lyon. Their captain feared that if he took them 170 miles north to Chesapeake, they would not have time to head back to England before the onset of hurricane season. None of them knew that the natives had been antagonized by the previous military occupants, during the earlier, failed visit there. So, they were in a place hostile to the new colonists and at a time too late in the season for planting. They were thus in need of support from the natives but this was difficult to achieve. They were able to connect with a different, more friendly tribe, south of Roanoke Island, the Roatan, and it was on them that their hopes for survival depended. Governor White, seeing how desperate they were for supplies and provisions, returned to England to get the necessary supplies and quickly return. With an average sailing time of six weeks he would be fortunate to get back to England, secure the needed supplies, find a ship, and make the return much before Christmas. Weather would also be a factor not in his favor. Unfortunately, Queen Elizabeth commandeered all available ships to help stave off the Spanish fleet and he was unable to return for three years. When he did manage to make the trip back to Roanoke he found the colony deserted and no indication when or why. White and his men found no trace of the more than 100 colonists he left behind, and there was no sign of violence. The only clue to their disappearance was the word "CROATOAN" carved into the palisade that had been built around the settlement. The assumption was that the colonists had moved to Croatoan Island, some 50 miles farther south. Governor White did not attempt to find them. He turned back because of bad weather and returned to England without ascertaining their fate.

Unfortunately for the 117 stranded colonists their numbers were too great for the friendly local natives to sustain over the winter. The natives barely had enough for themselves, it having been a dry year. Their crops did not do well, and game animals were scarce. Fish and shellfish were plentiful enough but did not form a huge part of their diet.

The only effective solution was to parcel them out in smaller groups to other friendly tribes in the region so there would be some chance for survival. Many of them had knowledge and skills the natives could put to use but others were gentlemen, unused to physical labor, who had only made the journey for the promised land grants and whatever riches to be found there, like gold and silver being mined by the Spanish far to the south. They would be put to work or banished if they proved not worth their keep.

With Fall upon them and winter approaching there was a sense of urgency among the practical minded of them but there were many opinions about what they should do and therefore many factions formed amongst them. Some wanted to make the long journey to Chesapeake, their original destination. Some wanted to stay with the Croatans, the friendly natives fifty miles south on Croatoan Island and wait for Governor White to return. Others wanted to move out on their own to explore and find their own way to riches. Still others yearned for the more comfortable company of Europeans and desired to go south to meet up with whatever Spanish colony they could find. Intertwined with all these different agendas was the inescapable fact that there were only seventeen women for eighty-seven men, which created social tensions, arguments, and in-fighting. The nine single females had formed attachments during their sea voyage but these were vigorously challenged. The ten children, one born on the ship and one after arrival, also needed to be a priority. One newborn, Virginia Dare, the daughter of Ananias and Elynor Dare, granddaughter of the Governor, was the first English person born in America.

Only a few of the men could handle weapons or even had weapons, and only a few who knew enough about farming. Many had useful trades like smithing or building. Unfortunately, it was too late in the season for planting so they were dependent needed to find local support from the natives to make it through the winter. The flyboat being towed behind them had most of their supplies which were lost when they lost the flyboat not far out of Portsmouth. The captain of their ship was worried about the arrival of hurricane season and wanted desperately to begin the voyage home which was why they were deposited at first landfall, at Roanoke, and not Chesapeake. They also had only a limited supply of tools, not enough to go around, and their store of powder was limited, too, and lead. In fact, they were short of everything needed to sustain themselves through the winter. Important decisions had to be made, and quickly. This was not easy for them since they were used to their decisions being made for them and the few emergent leader personalities did not have the experience to argue any position effectively. Many sunk into a profound depression, not seeing any way out of their precarious situation. The occasional native attacks on them while out foraging only made matters worse. Virtually all of them expressed how sorry they were for agreeing to come on this ill-fated journey.

After a great deal of discussion, many arguments,

some violent, the women and gentlemen and many of the older men agreed they needed to leave Roanoke as soon as possible. Most were in favor of wintering over with the Croatan, on their island, if they will have them, and wait for Governor White's return. More than two-thirds of them were in favor of this option, which was too many for the one Croatan village to take on through the winter. These eighty-one people, including all the women and children, felt their highest priority was to stick together and await the Governor's return.

The thirty-six men who favored other courses of action talked long and hard about their options and decided that there were two worth acting on. First, they could strike out to the west, away from the ocean, seeking adventure along the way, staking their claims to land, taking life as it came at them. Second, they could head south toward the Spanish settlements down Florida way and make lives there or await transport back to Spain or anywhere on the Continent.

When put to a vote they divided themselves among these three options and after many, many hours of discussion they agreed to split their meager possessions among the three groups and they felt some urgency because summer had turned to early fall and they all wanted to have some shelter before the winter set in.

The first step was to leave Roanoke and the deadly threat of the local natives. The Roatans who were willing to guide the more than 100 colonists to their island could not accept more than twenty additional mouths to feed. The group was therefore divided into smaller groups of no more than a dozen and they were parceled out to various friendly villages up and down the coast, but away from the hostiles. Men stayed with their wives and children and many single men opted to stay with the groups waiting for the Governor's return.

They began dividing their meager provisions among the three different groups. Their books and records were put in chests and hidden in the woods to be recovered by Gov. White when he returned. They divided up their weapons and powder and shot, tools, food, seeds, clothing, canteens, cooking utensils.

The groups striking out on their own decided not to take seeds, or heavy cooking utensils, but tin cups were desired. They wanted more than their fair share of the powder and shot, and swords.

The group looking for the Spanish knew they had many weeks of hard travel ahead of them so wanted to travel light and live off the land.

Discussions about all this had raged for days, all the while food became even scarcer and winter became nearer. As discussions dragged on there were ever more frequent skirmishes with the local natives, and more violent arguments amongst the colonists. Two of the men were killed fighting over the women and duly buried, deeply, in the sandy soil with no markers lest the heathen natives dig them up and defile them. Delegations sent to talk to the natives met with no success. Peace was not an option for these people. As the weather got colder and the local natives ever more hostile it became evident that they could not winter over at the Palisades in any sort of safety. A hunting party of seven men and their weapons never returned. As an interim move they immediately went to live with the Roatan on Roatoan island, and carved that name on the Palisade at Roanoke. The local natives let them go safely because they were escorted by the Roatans, and because they were glad to see the last of them. The party now numbered 81 men, 17 woman, and 10 children, for a total of 104 souls.

The Roatan chief determined that this large number was unsupportable, and that they could only stay a few days. He also said that other tribes in the region he had parlayed with could take two hands of people each, as could the Roatan, provided they work hard and earn their keep. The 18 men who wanted to go south to find the Spanish decided to leave immediately, in a day or two, desiring to reach warmer weather to the south before the winter really set in. It is now late September, 1587. A party of warriors from the hostile native tribe have followed them to keep watch on their movements in case they decided to return to Roanoke.

The first to leave Roatan were the nine younger, more adventurous men, who wanted to strike out west on their own. They sneaked away in the night, taking more than their fair share of guns and powder, and shot. Their absence was noted the next morning and a Roatan tribesman offered to track them down and bring them back. He returned three days later only to report that all nine had been ambushed and killed by their enemies from Roanoke. None of their weapons or supplies were found on or with their bodies. These young men, full of confidence in their superior weapons, and the fact that there were nine of them, did not think they were likely to suffer harm in any attack by these natives. But by this time the natives understood that their muskets, while loud and scary, took some time to reload. They also understood that their swords and sabers were of little use in dense woods. The natives with their bows and arrows, stealth, and knowledge of the woods, had all the advantages and used them to best effect. It was short work to ambush and cut down these arrogant foreign invaders although they did lose one of their number to gunshot and another was badly wounded. The rest of the guns were either being carried on slings or were unloaded and one misfired. The natives were correct about the swords and cutlasses. Easy to shoot them with arrows from a distance while out of range of these weapons.

When word of their fallen comrades spread through the twenty-seven men who favored the Spanish option, tenuous at first, began to think that was looking better and better. The only problem was safe passage on their way south. They sent their Croatan native friend to parlay with the natives at Roanoke and he came back with word that they agreed to let them go if they promised to never return. This was easy for them to agree on and so four days later eighteen of the men began the long trek south to find a Spanish settlement in Florida. They had no idea how far away that was but they thought the farther the better given the hostile nature of the local natives.

The eighty-one remaining colonists, consisting

of the Dare family and most of the gentlemen with no survival skills and a few young, able-bodied men and their wives, sweethearts and children were moved to four villages in the region in addition to Roatoan Island. This made the numbers more manageable and they were able to visit each other from time to time. Everyone agreed, English and Native, that this was the right thing to do at least through the winter after which the situation could be revisited. It was felt by Ananias Dare and a few other of the men that they might want to strike out for Chesapeake the following summer after their supplies arrived. There they thought they could build suitable shelter and live off the bounty of the marshes, with the fish, shellfish, and waterfowl, as well as the turkeys and deer that abounded in the woods. All they had to do is survive this winter. And perhaps the Governor might return at any time so watch must be kept for that, too. They had let the Governor know where at least one group had gone by carving the word "Roatoan" on one of the palisades at Roanoke. Since they had found friendly natives to help them survive Ananias felt that the cross above the name would have given a wrong impression.

There is no evidence that the group bound for Florida and the Spanish settlements, ever arrived. They were ill equipped for the journey to start with and had few of the survival skills necessary for such a journey. The many swamps took their toll, as did native hunting parties, as did sickness, and finally starvation. To their credit, a few of them managed to get as far as three hundred miles south before the last of them perished and no record was ever recovered from them as no journals or other evidence was found. As people died they were placed in shallow graves with only some sticks or stones for markers. The last to die simply decomposed above ground like any dead animal.

The group that remained to wait for Governor White's return found that the weather was milder than it would have been at home in England that time of year but not by much and fortunately there was little rainfall. Game was plentiful and the natives were adept at trapping rabbit and squirrel and other small game, as well as deer, of which there were many. The men only shot at deer when they could get very close to save their precious powder and balls. Once that was all used up there would be no more use for the muskets and so any miss was a tragedy. The Englishmen learned how to make bows and arrows and the men worked diligently to get proficient with them. Bowmen in England were famous but none of these colonists had ever used that weapon before. Also, this was a different kind of bow and a different environment in which to use it. Shooting an arrow in any thick woods is problematic because of the foliage that deflects the missile and then the arrow is difficult to find, and they are not easy to fabricate. This group in total had two axes, one saw, three hatchets, two cutlasses, one sword, three muskets, five horns of powder, and two pounds of lead for making shot in their one mold. They had managed to keep one five pound bag of beans dry and free of mold and weevils. They had no flour, two pounds of salt, a few potatoes almost black now, and a few wild onions. They had one cook pot which stayed with the Dare family. It was their prized possession. Everyone was down to a single wardrobe. Many of them took to wearing native dress in order to save their English clothing for the colony they would later build. There were insufficient blankets for everyone so they did their best to secure animal skins and stitch them together. Rabbit was plentiful and soon everyone had some sort of rabbit fur vest or coat or blanket. They gathered leaves to augment their crude pallets for sleeping and bugs were a scourge on their itchy skins. The natives helped them make fishing rods and the women provided the string needed to attach the hooks someone had the foresight to bring with them. Their string was not designed for continuous fishing and when it broke the hooks were lost. They were shown all the various survival skills the natives used and took quickly to spearing frogs and catfish and flounder from the many streams and pools in the area. Because they had native hovels to sleep in they did not build English style shelter, especially considering that they were likely moving to Chesapeake in the coming year. They set themselves to work, men and women and the older children, as if they were natives themselves. They shared information and the English became more and more adept at speaking the local languages of the natives. Each village it seemed had its own dialect of a common tongue.

That winter one child died of unknown causes and one of fever. Four of the gentlemen in the group, unused to any physical labor, proved to be completely useless and were denied food until they pitched in and helped the women at least with their gathering of wood for fires and water for cooking and cleaning. Ananias threatened them with execution if they did not lend a hand with the men. One of them did try to help with wood cutting but the ax he was unaccustomed to using bounced off a log and into his shin. Not only was this painful but the wound festered and he died from it after a week of suffering.

When things were especially bad they turned to prayer and they read their bible aloud at night around the warm fire. The Christmas of +1587 UAY was a grim one indeed for English accustomed to warm homes and traditional hot meals and warm clothing. They all worked hard to survive a very difficult winter but recognized that their hosts had it no better than they did and suffered the same aches and pains, hard work, with sometimes too little to eat or to do. With the Roatan, little Virginia remained healthy through this first winter, and Elynor and Ananias were forever praying it would continue. She was a model child with flaming red hair and green eyes. The natives gave her the name "Shining Star" because of her smile and her unusual beauty. Once she was finished with nursing she seemed to thrive on native food. Their mixed diet of meat, seafood, and vegetables suited her. Elynor would chew meat and other foods to soften them before giving it to Virginia, as the natives did with their own children. The need for human companionship was keen during the short winter days and long nights. The Roatan group, with the Dare family, remained on Roatoan, close by the coast to ensure they would see any English ship come to call, and where they had told Governor White or any Englishmen, where they had gone from Roanoke. They did not see the others all winter but heard from their hosts that they were content where they were. It was noted that two children had died from a fever, as did six of their own children and three English adults. During the long cold nights the Dare group, numbering twelve people, spent a great deal of time together in the now crowded village communal hut. The English read from the bible and the natives were entranced by that. Words they did not understand coming out of a book they did not have any concept of were somehow soothing to them. The English also sang songs and had made some crude musical instruments, a flute and a sort of harp out of dried gut. The music was by no means polished but the natives were entranced by that as well. The women shared stories of their lives as their language skills improved and in this way the English bonded with the natives in all their villages.

In late April, +1588 UAY, the area was exploding with the colors of the fresh season, and all of the colonists except the Dare group were moved inland with the annual migration of their villages to the western foothills. The Dare family and close friends remained in the area awaiting the return of Governor White. This marked a distinct separation of those colonists who wanted to reunite with Governor White and continue on to Chesapeake. The Dares lost all direct contact with them and only ever heard stories about them from their native hosts. Ananias was told that the others understood they were being relocated to a large village which could accommodate them all and they would be with a tribe far from their enemies who were better able to care for them. They journeyed south and west for some two weeks through magnificent forests, along ancient game trails, teeming with all manner of animals and birds and insects. When they arrived in the foothills of a beautiful mountain range they were taken to a very substantial village and told that this was their new home. The Dares never saw them again but were confident they were better off than trying to fend off enemy natives or build their own settlement.

The Dares and their small group of friends from England continued to hope through the year +1588 UAY that John White would return with the promised supplies and kept a vigil along the coast and their hosts checked on Roanoke from time to time. He never appeared and they went into the winter season feeling better about their lives than the previous winter but wondering what happened to their governor. The same thing repeated itself for the year 1589 and 1590. By this time Virginia was three years old and walking, talking, and doing all the things children do at her age when living a stone-age life on a distant continent. She spoke the Roatan dialect of their Iroquoian language and was totally a young native American except for her white skin, pale hair, and green eyes. Ananias and Elynor Dare were proud of her and proud of their assimilation into the tribe of the Roatan. They missed England of course and missed their other friends who had relocated to the Carolina foothills. In September 1590, after a severe storm in late August, the Dares and their group decided to join their party in the Carolinas and their hosts agreed to start them on their journey. None or their hosts had been able to visit Roanoke because of the storm so missed the arrival of Governor White, who left shortly after arriving because of the approaching storm. Ships of that era did not fare well in hurricane conditions and avoided them at all costs.

Considering their journey to rejoin the remainder of the colonists their native hosts explained that they would accompany them south for a hand of days till they reached the next village on the path. They would then hand them off to the various friendly tribes along the well-traveled route and it would take them perhaps a full moon to reach them. The Roatan held a modest feast to honor them as they departed and they all hugged Shining Star, whom they considered the luck of their village, and something of a goddess.

The weather was favorable, but the route was obscured by the damage from the recent hurricane. Their guides helped them all stay on the correct trails and helped them with food and shelter along way. It took them one hand longer than a moon to reach their friends, what was left of the original colonists unceremoniously dropped off at Roanoke Island. Ananias did a formal muster the day after their arrival. He counted seventy-two survivors, in total, from the 117 who began this ill-fated journey. Of course the sixty survivors in the Carolina village wanted to know what happened to Governor White and Ananias told them he could only assume he had been lost at sea with his resupply ship, and could not say why no other relief vessel had some to save them. They all knelt and prayed, to the astonishment of their native hosts, who stood by quietly while these pale people, so far from their homes, prayed to their unseen gods.

As fantastic as it may seem, Governor White did not expend much energy trying to find his daughter, her husband and his granddaughter, before or after the storm. He seemed to leave for England too hastily for someone three years overdue on his promise to return with supplies. He also seems to have been completely irresponsible in not moving heaven and earth to find his abandoned his family and his entire colony. He left no clues in his diaries or in his known letters to friends or benefactors beyond his confidence that they had all been safely ensconced with the friendly natives of Roatoan. Clearly there was more to it than that. With no Vid-Watch club following the story there was no purposeful surveillance coverage of the man or his colony. There were minimal static and a few dynamic surveillance bots gathering information for later anonymous use and they are the only sources of information on the entirety of these events. Inferences drawn from things he said on the return supply voyage in 1590 might indicate his involvement in some political maneuvering in Elizabeth's court, intertwined with competition between Sir Walter Raleigh and Sir Francis Drake for the Queen's favor. These events seem to have been the reason for his three-year delay in returning to his colony at Roanoke and also seem to have caused his less than eager desire to find the colony. His journal entry expressing his relief that the colony had moved with the friendly natives to Croatoan seemed to be justification for abandoning then and returning to England. That can only be speculated on of course since there is no evidence of definitive reasoning on this issue.

In the Spring of 1591, the colonists, now under the leadership of Ananias Dare, held a formal meeting, wearing what English clothing that had survived. The purpose of the meeting was to discuss then take a vote on what they wanted to do. Did they dare strike out north in hopes of reaching Chesapeake on the chance of finding passage back to England or south to meet up with the Spanish or did they want to stay where they were? When Ananias called for a show of hands on remaining with their native friends there in the foothills, he began to cry with emotion when he saw all their hands in the air. He knew, as they did, that they had a comfortable life with the natives, integrated as they now were into their society, and had no desire to chance a return sea voyage to England or even the arduous trek back to dangerous Roanoke or south to Florida. They never learned the fate of the party that went in search of the Spanish in Florida but wished them well and prayed for their safety.

A few of them, Virginia included, lived to hear of ships from England or other countries putting in along the coast in order to establish colonies in the early 1600s. Momentarily the older ones had pangs of homesickness and the desire to reach out to these kinsmen but at that time there was no easy way to travel the long distances involved and after whimsical discussion they always decided to let sleeping dogs lie. Virginia felt none of this nostalgia for England, having never seen it, and only hearing stories about it from time to time. Life there may have been different, but it seems it was no better. Of course, Virginia was not really English, in her heart or in fact, even if she did have fair skin, red hair, and green eyes. Born in this land, she had lived her entire life with the natives and considered herself one. When she was fifteen she married the son of a local clan chief and had three sons and lived a happy, contented life with her adopted family. It did not matter to her that she looked different from the rest of them. She remarked often to her children that she did not feel any different.

In the summer of her thirty-seventh year the tribe was visiting their clan cousins on the coast and an English ship from the Indies put in to gather fresh water. Her family greeted the English warmly and Virginia had a chance to use her English, so seldom used now that her mother and father had passed. The English found her remarkable. She appeared in every respect an English woman, albeit deeply tanned, like Europeans who live year-round in the Indies. But clearly, she was a member of this native tribe, with her husband and children all natives. Virginia knew her history of course but did not mention it to these strangers lest they take a greater interest and perhaps even cause notice of her existence in England. She wanted to ask them why no one had come to rescue them after Governor White abandoned them and also burned to know what happened to Governor White but again, chose the cautious path and said nothing of these things. Her mother and father had filled her young head with stories of England and their voyage and her grandfather, the Governor but it all was second hand and had none of the urgency of an abandoned Englishman. She did not feel like one and never had. After two days ashore while the crew was laying on fresh water and what game and fish they could kill or capture, the English departed for home. That was the last time she was seen by any English person and the last time she saw anyone from England or Europe. She died at the age of sixty-one having lived a full and contented life. Her light-skinned sons mourned her passing in the way their ritual prescribed, tears forming in their green and grey and even blue eyes. Two of her three sons had auburn hair and one was coal black. They had learned to read English but did not speak it well. They often read to their tribe from the bible and from the one other book their mother kept after her parents died. Not much was gleaned from these readings but they helped pass the time on long, cold winter nights. Every now and then one of them would put on a shirt or pants of their father's. They also loved his boots. These things remained in the family until they rotted away over time.

Diary Number Eight

Following Objects Over Time – Thirty Pieces of Silver

Faculty Introduction. Some Vid-Watch clubs demand details of obscure events and it is the pride of our surveillance system on Earth that we are able to answer most of these demands. This diary shows you the utility of bot surveillance in historical research based on the vast extent of our surveillance system. Object recognition capability is a prominent feature of our surveillance applications. It enables rapid searches for items that have been accurately captured for file and can therefore be accurately located and used for comparison. As in this example, certain objects were anonymously recorded in great detail by Shonak's very effective surveillance sensors. This enabled searches of our extensive data files for recurrences of these objects as captured by any sensor anywhere in our system. That is how the analysts were able to reconstruct the movement of the coins in question. One of the more obscure of the Plus-Five Vid-Watch clubs on Shonak does research into what happened to things mentioned in popular histories by the Earthers themselves. Many of these things are associated with famous people and the various contemporary and later accounts of their lives and things associated with them. This is an account of the "Thirty Pieces of Silver" which the Earther Christian bible, New Testament, mentions in the book of Mathew, Chapter 26, verses 14-16: "Then one of the twelve, called Judas Iscariot, went to the chief priests (Rabbis) and said, "What are you willing to give me if I deliver Him to you?" And they counted out to him thirty pieces of silver. So, from that time he sought opportunity to betray Him."

At the request of this Vid-Watch club an attempt was made to trace the whereabouts of all these thirty pieces as of the year 2020 UAY, when the request was made. It took some cross-matching the results of multiple sensors of all types over a considerable period, but the following accounting is judged to be accurate to three decimal places. At this writing only one of the original thirty has survived. It is a tetra drachma from the fifth year of the reign of Ptolemy X, minted on Cyprus in the Earth year, -102 UAY.

Diary. Feeling flushed with his sudden wealth, Judas Escariot spread the coins out on his eating table where they were duly imaged by two static and one dynamic video sensor. At the time of course they were not considered any more important than food or wine he would have put on the same table. These sensors simply captured everything; such is the extent of Shonakian surveillance, even as far back as that. It was therefore possible, later, for Shonakian analysts in the Vid-Watch club doing this research, to accurately establish the beginning of the search, in the hands of Judas himself. The precise imaging was crucial for the later identification of these coins that appear in any Bot diary, anywhere or any time. Later, after the crucifixion, and feeling guilty and very ashamed, Judas Escariot returned the silver he received from the rabbis who had paid him to betray his friend, Jesus. Surveillance noted that these coins were placed in an empty clay pot and set aside. The rabbis considered these coins to be unclean "blood money"; directly linked to the execution of Jesus by the Romans. Over the next days, five of the coins were pilfered in secret by a less than pious rabbi as souvenirs but replaced with other coins of equal value. These pilfered coins were among the first to go missing from accountability as they were eventually spent by the rabbi's son who saw where his father had hidden them. This son did not know or care of their significance, only their value. One silver coin of that weight and stamp would support a family of four for a week in those times and so were not of trivial monetary value. His father did of course note that the coins were missing, and audibly cursed his fate, but as he had taken them illicitly himself, he could not make any fuss over it. He was fairly certain his son had taken them and squandered them, but he remained silent. As did his son, who left the house shortly thereafter, now having the money he needed to move out and start his own life free from his family's strict personal controls. He was heard bragging to his friends that he was destined for great things and was traveling to Alexandria to start a new life.

It was a triumph of Shonak's technology that the coins could be traced at all, but it required a clear image in order to do so. Object recognition was important for their historical research and since the original images of the coins spread out on Judas' table were of high quality, it only required another good image to determine a match for any of them. Unfortunately the coins spent by the Rabbi's son to make the move to Egypt was done in circumstances that did not allow for good images of them to be acquired by the many sensors he was in range of, and as a result they were lost to history. There were now twenty-five coins in play.

The eventual use of the remaining coins to purchase a local potter's field by the rabbis of Jerusalem, for the burial of the indigent and poor of the city, was considered by them to be a just way to rid themselves of this tainted money. They of course did not know that only twenty-five of the coins were "tainted" with the blood of Jesus.

The traceable twenty-five coins were given to the Roman Prefecture who governed the area and who owned the field. These coins were placed in the general coffers of the Romans, to be used for general commerce as needed, to pay merchants and the like for goods and services to the Roman garrison and government. One particularly keen Centurion assigned to the garrison there, Marcus Ficus, was interested in local history and local affairs, and was also avid coin collector. As Rome pillaged its way through the known world he was able to acquire coins from many different places. He specialized in coins with some unique story. For example, one of his coins in his collection came from the purse of an enemy chieftain Marcus personally killed in battle. The chief had many coins but Marcus only kept the one he liked the best and spent the rest on wine and food and whores. When he heard of the "thirty pieces of silver" paid to a friend of Jesus in order to betray him he was immediately interested in these coins. He was friends with one of the Romans in the treasury, a drinking buddy, and inquired after the coins that had been given for the field. The treasury custodian, Claudius Dimeter, had secured coins for his collection in the past so was familiar with Marcus' love of coins. Marcus greeted him warmly and pressing the requisite bribe into his hand, said he wanted to add some more coins to his collection. He said of course, as usual, he would replace any he took with coins of equal value. He told him he was eager to have some of the coins recently received from the rabbis when they bought the potter's field. Claudius remembered which pot he put the coins into, and they agreed to meet at the treasury the next day. Of course Marcus paid for the drinks all night.

When they met at the garrison treasury the next morning, Claudius took Marcus into the coin room and lifted a clay pot from a shelf and took it to the scale. He weighed it carefully then took it to the counting table and poured out the coins for Marcus' inspection. Centurion Ficus noted that there were perhaps a hundred coins in the pot and asked if there was anything special about the particular coins he wanted, the ones from the field purchase. He said he needed something to help him find them from amongst the others in the pot. Claudius said it shouldn't be too hard, because all of the coins were tetra drachma of the Ptolemy stamp. Ficus thanked him and began to sort through the coins. While he was spreading the coins out, separating the Ptolemy tetra drachma from the rest, the centurion of the treasury guard came in to see Claudius. He noticed another centurion at a counting table and asked Claudius who he was and what he was doing. Titus Quintium was a suspicious man, honest to a fault, but none too bright. He had, however, influential family connections in Rome and was well thought of by the Prefect. Claudius told him his friend, Centurion Marcus Ficus , was a coin collector and often came in and bought coins he wanted. He paid for them with his own coins of equal value, duly certified before he was allowed to leave. Titus frowned. Coin collecting was not something Titus ever considered as worthwhile but went into the room and greeted Marcus, letting him know that he was the Treasury's Centurion. "Well met, then, Titus, look at these coins, are they not magnificent?" Titus glanced at them and smiled, thinking not of their beauty but rather of their value. He was wondering how he could benefit from what he was witnessing but paused to watch Marcus search for the coins he said he was looking for. The coins were nicely spread out on the large flat table for good viewing. This enabled the visual sensors in the room to acquire excellent images, and the twenty-five coins in question were clearly identified on that table. Marcus explained to Titus what he was looking for but found that unfortunately there were more than thirty of the coins in question in the pile. He also noted that the coins were of much higher value than he had anticipated and could not purchase them all anyway, all thirty, which was a king's ransom to him, and to Titus, as well. While Titus watched, Marcus carefully selected thirty coins he thought might be the ones and said he could only buy ten of them, as that was all the money he brought with him. This caused Titus to raise an eyebrow, for any centurion who could buy ten of these coins was rich indeed. Marcus anticipated his question and said that he had been lucky in his battles to acquire much bounty so was able to indulge his passion for coin collecting. Vid-Watch club analysis showed that he had selected eight of the coins he was eager to have, out of the ten he wanted to buy. He said again that the coins were of much higher value than he had thought and was disappointed he could buy no more than the ten he had selected. As tempting as it was to steal some, he knew that with Titus there it would not be possible and he would be crucified himself, like Jesus, were he to do so. So he bought the ten coins, which was a small fortune for him, but he came prepared and managed. He replaced the remaining coins into the pot, and Claudius the treasurer, who had been watching him the whole time, as had centurion Titus, put Marcus' payment into the pot and weighed it again. He was satisfied that it was of equal weight, and thanked Marcus for his continued honesty, and bid him a good day. The treasurer did not care about the individual coins themselves, just the silver weight, and therefore the value, of those in his charge.

Once outside the treasury, Titus stopped Marcus and said he had reservations about the legality of what he just witnessed. He told Marcus he could make trouble for him unless they could come to some accommodation. Marcus stared at him long and hard but in the end realized that Titus was the Treasury Centurion and could indeed make great trouble for him. Fear is a great motivator and so Marcus reached into his pouch and took out one of the ten coins. He placed it in his palm and held it out to Titus, and in doing this the coin was duly imaged by Shonakian sensors. It was one of the true coins. Titus took the coin, tapped the side of his nose with two fingers, smiled, and said, "You are welcome in the treasury any time, my friend, just be sure I am there with you." Marcus frowned, and as Titus walked away, out of earshot, Marcus mumbled to himself that this would then be the last time he ever used the treasury as a place to find nice coins for his collection. Marcus walked back to his home with nine new coins, seven of which were the true coins. The remaining seventeen "blood money" coins in the treasury were subsequently lost to history as they were simply spent and dispersed in the area with no record of where any particular coins went. Most of the silver coins in the treasury with foreign stamps were in fact routinely melted down into ingots to supply the local coin stamper with the raw material from which to fashion Roman coins of various denominations. Titus, our centurion who managed to secure one of the true coins from Marchs, did not have his very long. He went to a local brothel and spent the coin on two days of debauchery. At the end of his stay he left with a hangover but not with any money. The owner of the brothel must have held onto the coin for months because it was not imaged again until some months later when it was imaged being used for the purchase of clothing for the ladies of the establishment. One of the cloth merchants received the coin but on his way home it fell through a hole in his pocket, rolled into the street, where it was nicely wedged between stones. It has never been imaged again and is perhaps still there.

In the years that followed the Centurion who possessed the last seven coins of "the thirty" treasured them and kept them safe. Of course he thought he had nine of the coins. When his posting in Jerusalem was at an end, he was transferred to Gaul to help defend Rome against their enemies there and to keep order. He kept his coin collection with him, as it consisted of many items dear to him, but none dearer than the ones associated with the betrayal of Jesus. Eventually, almost inevitably,

Marcus Ficus was severely wounded in a skirmish with some northern tribesmen and was invalided out of active service. His pension was insufficient to maintain his lifestyle and reluctantly he sold off the booty he had acquired over his active service, some of which had considerable value. As the years went by he moved to warmer climes in southern Gaul and gradually sold off all his booty except for his special coins from Jerusalem. Near the end of his life it was necessary to sell even those coins and he found a buyer he could trust to give him maximum value. It was in the year +43 UAY that the old Centurion told the coin merchant the story of the coins for the betrayal of Jesus of Nazareth. Jesus was not yet the famous religious figure he would be later, but the buyer had heard of him during his travels. He was happy to buy all nine of the coins at a price higher than the weight called for, but the Centurion kept one for himself, a particularly nice specimen. He held it up to the light and turned it over and over allowing multiple sensors to capture it in detail.

When reviewing that video, the vid club was able to determine that it was one of the original thirty. The buyer examined the remaining eight tetra drachma coins before he purchased them, spreading them out on an animal skin to do so. Satisfied with their silver content, he met the Centurion's price, bundled the coins into the skin, and put them in a chest in his cart. He gathered his guards, who were resting in the shade, and departed with eight of Pontius' coins, six of which were genuinely "Christ's Blood" coins. Early the next year the Centurion died but, on his deathbed, he gave his last tetra drachma to his good friend Gaius, with whom he was sharing his home. He told Gaius the story behind his purchase, so many years earlier in Jerusalem.

It is at this point the coin trail splits into two branches. The first being with the coin merchant who bought eight of the coins, six of them original "blood" coins, and the second being the Centurion's friend, who also now had one of the real coins.

The merchant's trail was a short one. He was traveling with his horse-drawn cart and two loyal guards. Stopping each night for rest and to eat, usually in a campsite but sometimes at a farmhouse or a common room on a main road. The Romans made superior roads and when you found one you tended to stay on it as long as it continued in the general direction you were headed. The common rooms or inns along these roads were convenient and dry, and normally had people on the floor on bedrolls or cots and places for horses to be fed and watered. As it happened the weather in the Spring of Year +44 UAY was particularly violent, with strong winds and heavy rain. Streams rushing down the mountain sides in southern Gaul were swollen with rain and snow melt, washing out roads, uprooting trees, and noisily raging down the mountains with considerable violence. On this evening the weather was particularly harsh. The merchant and team were on a good road, but in windswept, blinding rain, looking for any place to find shelter. As it happened, neither the merchant, who was driving, or the old horse, both blinded by the wind and rain coming directly into their faces, did not see the sharp curve that led to the bridge and they stumbled straight ahead into the raging torrent coming down the ravine. The horse and cart tumbled in, to be lost instantly downstream, banging from boulder to boulder as the water crashed down on them, splintering the cart and crushing the horse and merchant, drowning them both. The cargo was smashed and lost as well. The two guards, sitting on the back of the cart, were caught in the fall but one guard managed to jump off just before it went into the gorge. Hanging onto a tree root, he dimly saw in the violent storm that all the rest were lost to the torrent. It was only due to luck and to his superior reflexes that this one drowsing guard had been able to escape the fate of his fellows. He was Pontius Durinis and had been a Legionary soldier of "first spear" talent and courage. For people who know combat in that era, any soldier who survived multiple battles after being in the front line of attack, the first spear, was both highly skilled and also very lucky. He was smart enough to know that eventually his luck would run out no matter how brave or skilled he was, so he left the army as soon as he could do so on good report, and hired himself out as a guard. He expected more money, better food, fewer people yelling at him, and far less danger. Up until now, that had been the case. Mourning the loss of his friend, he crawled up from the abyss, through the mud and rain, to some rocks by the road and pulled his cloak over himself before he fell asleep. The last words he muttered for the sensors to catch, as he drifted off to exhausted sleep, was that he might as well be back in the Legion if the gods were going to treat him this way.

In the morning he was shaken awake by a man who asked after his health. Without thinking, Pontius grabbed the man by his cloak and threw him to the ground, taking the man's knife out of his belt on his way down, and placing it across his throat. The man screamed and begged for his life and Pontius, realizing this man was just a weary traveler like himself, let him go and then helped him to his feet, with apologies. He explained that he had been a soldier and his training got the better of him before he was fully awake. The traveler, still shaken, and with a shallow cut on his neck, gathered himself and grudgingly accepted Pontius' apology. Pontius explained what had happened and although cold, wet, and sore from his experience of the previous night limped over to the ravine to see if there was any sign of his companions. He saw a wheel from the cart, caught in a thick, twisted pile of broken branches, but could see nothing of his fellow guard, a friend of ten years, or the merchant, or his horse, or his wagon. He did not tell the stranger what their business was, merely that he had been with two others and a horse and a cart that had been taken by the violent stream. The stranger offered his condolences and also a piece of bread and cheese, for sparing his life, and because he knew this man would sorely need something to eat after experiencing so much. The stranger then bid Pontius farewell and walked away, crossing the bridge which he was just now noticing. "What an idiot that horse was" he shouted to the sky and to no one in particular. He buried his face in his hands thinking how cruel their fate had been, especially that idiot old horse and the two other men. Sullen then, and in bad humor, and sore, Pontius ate the food and stayed there until the torrent subsided enough for him to start looking for his friend. Perhaps he had managed to grab onto something too? He walked downstream along the bank of the ravine for an hour, looking for evidence of the cart or horse or master or his friend. He could see nothing but uprooted trees and branches and mud, and boulders. He returned to where the wheel was caught in the tangle of branches and tree roots near where the bridge met the bank of the ravine. It was difficult footing getting out there; the wood was still wet and slippery, with spray from the torrent just below him. He had to crawl as his hands were much better at gripping the tangled wood than his sandaled feet. The water was still rushing by, but much less fiercely, and he kept at it. He was fearful of falling in but looked for anything he could possibly scavenge from the cart, if anything survived. There was food in the cart, and wine, and of course the coin chests and other treasures. Perhaps something of all that could be found. Digging down through the branches by the wheel he spied a bit of wet burlap cloth of the type that the merchant wrapped his boxes in. After half an hour of tugging and removing branches from the massive tangle, while balancing on the pile, he was able to drag the bundle out. It was very heavy, which likely was why it stuck where it landed as the cart tipped into the water. To his delight he found that it was one of the coin chests the merchant had packed away. He was hoping it was the gold chest but alas when he opened it he saw only silver. He could see there were possibly ten hands worth of coins in there. He would be able to live quite nicely for some time on this bounty. What he did not know anything about was that six "true" blood money coins were in this chest he had recovered. Pontius carefully took the coins out of the chest, which he could not easily carry on foot, and in any event would be too conspicuous. He had no weapon and no protection from thieves that prowled the roads, so he tossed the empty chest into the stream to see it smash to pieces and get borne away by the water. He wrapped the coins in the burlap to make them less conspicuous and tied them securely around his waist, under his torn, dirty tunic. He continued throughout the day to search in the brambles and branches for more bounty but found nothing. He did manage to find a suitable piece of driftwood to serve as both walking stick and weapon should that be needed. The way he was dressed no one would suspect him of being a first spear Legionary, or a man of new-found wealth. He spent the night there and set out in the morning across the bridge and down the road. He walked for days, eating berries and mushrooms, drinking from the stream, until he came to a small settlement where he was able to purchase some food and wine. The few people there did not think him worth bothering about as he was poorly dressed, filthy, and clearly not someone with anything to steal. He also carried himself well and looked fit enough to handle himself in a fight. He rested there for two days, disappearing into the woods to stay out of notice, and eating what he could find. He wanted to get to a garrison town with some law and order before he tried to use his new wealth. He even begged for food from the strangers he met along the way. It took him seven days for him to reach a Roman garrison town by which time he was exhausted, all but done in, really. He wearily approached the garrison, told the officer of the watch his name, that he was a Roman citizen, and a merchant who had been caught in the recent storm. He recounted the story of the wagon going into the swollen stream, which helped explain his torn, dirty appearance. He then deposited his treasure with them, taking a receipt for it, thanking the gods for the Romans in this gods-forsaken part of the Empire. He kept a few of the smaller silver coins to keep him until he figured out his next move. He found a place to take a warm bath, to purchase new clothes and food, and a gladius for protection. He found a comfortable bed, too, and spent four nights there, resting and learning as much about where he was that he could. Then he could decide where he would go next. He was determined to find a village to settle in near the southern coast of Gaul. He retrieved his money from the garrison and paid a merchant to let him ride in his wagon as he travelled south on that wonderful Roman road, carrying six of the silver coins used to betray Jesus. He knew nothing about that, but he did know those coins had considerable value as they were reverently handled by the merchant after he bought them now some two weeks earlier. As he made his way along the coast of Gaul, along the Mare Nostrum, he found a village to settle in and he used the coins to finance the purchase of a small cottage and the setting up of a forge, thinking he would be a smith, like his father. He sold all of the coins to a jeweler who melted them down so he could work the silver into items for sale to the wealthy Romans who lived in the area. All six of the Thirty in Pontius' possession were thus melted down and lost to history.

Meanwhile, the Centurion's friend, Clovis Arminius, who had the one remaining piece of the infamous "thirty pieces of silver" in his possession, married a local widow and subsequently told his family, several times over the years, the story his friend told him about his coin. In time this last of the coins passed to the oldest stepson who was a successful smith. He decided to wear the coin around his neck and mounted it nicely, avoiding drilling a hole in it as so many others might have done. This smith wore the treasured family heirloom under his clothes so as not to attract attention to it but admired it, along with his family, when they were alone inside their home. Many high-quality sensor images over the years confirm this coin's provenance. The coin eventually passed to Clovis' step-grandson along with the family history, when it was time for him to divest of worldly possessions. The coin remained in the family for then many generations to the year +415 UAY when it passed into the possession of a thief and murderer who, along with his band of criminals, raided and plundered homes and villages in this area of Gaul.

It was a time of general lawlessness as the Romans found themselves stretched beyond capacity with an empire too big to protect. The rule of law was replaced by the rule of the sword now in so many places where there was small threat of Roman army retaliation for misdeeds. This thief was attracted to the coin, ripped from the dead body of the smith wearing it, and to him it meant two things. First, it meant he had a prize of obvious beauty and value and second, it meant he was victor over the previous owner, whose home and family were destroyed and burned. He did not keep it long, however, as an even stronger and more brutal man than he was beat him to death when he was drunk on wine and then stripped his body of everything of value. This man was surprised to find something of such value around the neck of such a useless person in so humble a place but pleased to have the beautiful silver coin around his own neck. He considered himself far more worthy of such a thing than the loud-mouthed son of a whore's carcass he killed and robbed and said so repeatedly. The coin remained with this terrible human being until he was killed in ambush by the local lord's guards. The guard chief appropriated the coin who shortly lost it to the lord when it came to his attention. This lord was able to hold onto it until he died, and his son took it for himself. By this time, it needed to be re-mounted and the new owner was able to afford a silver mount carefully crafted so as not to harm the coin itself. The year is now +426 UAY and the coin is given as part of a dowry to another lord on the betrothal of the owner's daughter to the richer lord's son. This family, who owned vast tracts of land in Southern Gaul, home of the Visigoths, was prosperous and educated and proved good custodians of their wealth, including this last of the blood coins, of which they knew nothing. In the year +430 UAY this coin, along with other silver coins and objects, was placed in a large chest of twenty-stone weight and stored in the vaults in the bottom of their castle. These vaults, carved out of the native limestone of the hill the castle was on, were very secure. Lords of the castle came and went over the years and the family's wealth increased and diminished according to the stewardship of the families. Marriages, wars, gambling, drink, all impacted the wealth of the various landowners over the next centuries and yet the chest of silver remained untouched, and indeed, unnoticed by many of the lords of the castle. One former lord had covered that vault with rock, making it look like it was debris from carving it out, and after generations this knowledge was lost which of course meant the chest with the coin inside survived both feast and famine, fire and battles, births and deaths as the years rolled on.

In their year +925 UAY, in what was by then the Kingdom of the Francs, the lord of that particular land and castle was eager to renovate and expand the keep. He ordered a general survey of the entire structure and it was during this inspection that the rubble was removed from the vault chamber and the chest of silver was discovered, along with other things which had lain there undisturbed for some five centuries. The lord was informed and then examined the unexpected treasure. He found many items to use in his new castle and jewelry for his wife and daughters, and for some of his friends. He gave his son leave to take anything he pleased and his eye immediately fell on the blood coin. He just saw a beautiful work of coin art. He had no way of knowing it was a Greek Tetra Drachma with the head of Alexander, minted in the year -102 UAY, during the reign of Ptolemy X, and part of the blood money used to betray Jesus Christ. This son was educated and could read the Greek on the reverse of the coin and understood its history, then, of a sort, and determined to keep this coin for himself, along with a few other bits and baubles. He took it to the family jeweler who mounted it nicely for him to wear with a bold silver chain from that same chest. His father, when he saw it around his son's neck, took it for himself, promising the son would inherit it when he inherited everything else. This lord then wore the coin frequently, and the son liked how it looked, and eventually the son did inherit the coin and wore it daily with great satisfaction. In their year +933 UAY the son and his hunting party were set upon by roving bandits. The bandits, simply on their way through this area, immediately saw a great target of opportunity for rich plunder and attacked without hesitation. They outnumbered the lord and his party and the deed was quickly done, but not before the lord and his men acquitted themselves well, killing three of the bandits before falling to their greater numbers. The bandits hurriedly stripped everything of value from their victim, taking their horses, and a great deal of money pouches and jewelry, along with weapons and clothing. Realizing after the heat of battle the trouble they were in they then rode northeast for seventeen days to escape the inevitable sheriff's posse looking to avenge their lord. This is how the coin made its way from southern France to the northeast and Alsace. Here the bandits remained, spending their bounty away from people who would recognize any of it or who had heard of the attack. The bandit leader, who had taken to wearing the lord's coin, as they referred to it, passed out, drunk, in the bed of a woman he has just met. Her burly husband, returning early from a trip, flew into a wild rage upon finding a strange man in his bed. He killed the bandit with a dagger shoved into his brain from below his chin. His wife was standing next to the bed, screaming, so he beat her till she quieted down and then sat down himself. The dead man was still wearing the coin around his neck and the wife, trying to find a way to change her husband's dangerous mood, took the coin off the body and put it over the husband's head to fall nicely on his heaving chest. He looked at her, still glassy eyed from the shock and exertion of the past moments and told her to get rid of the body and bring him some food and drink. Not that he needed more strong drink, she could see he had had more than a little before stumbling home, but she hastened to comply.

In the following days the merchant became more and more attached to the beautiful coin around his neck and took it out often to admire its beauty. At first he had thought to sell it but now it had become his prized possession. His new coin necklace, with its heavy silver chain and the bold figure on the front of it was as unusual in this part of the world as it was around the neck of someone like him. He did not know it was Alexander, of course, nor did he understand the coin was Greek, and certainly did not know that it was one of the "thirty pieces of silver" mentioned by their priest during the story of the crucifixion. He wore it for the rest of his life and when he passed his wife took to wearing it herself. When she passed, childless, the coin and all her possessions went to her younger sister. This sister did not live in Alsace, but rather in a village near Paris, so it was carted off to her along with all the other portable things she owned, in due course. The year is now +962 UAY and the coin finds itself in Paris, where it was sold to an antiquary named Monsieur Henri Delacour, by the sister who was more interested in what she could get for her sister's belongings than any of the belongings themselves.

M. Delacour was a keen collector of coins of all sorts from all over the known world and recognized the coin instantly as being a fine example of Ptolemaic coinage. He placed it in a drawer with others of the same type he had collected over the years and there it sat until the man decided to sell up and retire to his villa outside Paris. In +980 UAY, in ill health, and in somewhat of a hurry, he gathered his gold and silver pieces coins and jewelry items of intrinsic value and put them in chests and auctioned it all off for what he could get, which was quite a lot, at least in his mind. Those chests then passed from merchant to merchant and bank to bank for the next seven hundred and six years. Every now and then, to prove the weight and contents, the chests were opened and usually consolidated with other like items, like coins with coins and plate with plate, and jewelry with jewelry, all of like metals of course, like gold with gold and silver with silver. Over this time gems were removed from many gold and silver items. It was at these times that the coin of our interest was noted by Shonakian sensors. The coin was removed from its silver mount and set aside. The gold and silver jewelry was then melted down or sold individually which happened to many of the coins, too. The gems were placed in their own chests.

In their year +1668 UAY, the King of France at the time, Louis XIV, concluded his war with Spain and some brief peace was realized. There was a good deal of land in the north of France and southern Dutch holdings that was changing hands as a result of the peace agreements among the various major and minor kingdoms and duchies, and fortunes were both won and lost. The owner of the chest of silver containing the coin we are following found it necessary to pay off heavy debts and had his various treasure chests broken open to begin the process of assessing their worth and making payments. His steward had the task of opening the chests and cataloguing their contents, and when he saw the "blood coin", not knowing its history of course, but admiring its beauty, quietly slipped it into his vest pocket and did not enter it in the list of contents. This act was duly captured by several well-placed Shonakian sensors. In this way the coin was separated from the hoard it had rested in safely for all those years and once again saw the light of day - though mostly it was kept in the steward's desk, in a small hidden drawer. He was reluctant to bring it out lest his employer notice it by some chance and surmise he had pilfered it somehow. He knew he should tell his employer or sell it, anything to prevent his theft being discovered, but he found that, for whatever reason, he loved the coin too much to do so.

This steward took sick in the year +1673 UAY and died, with the coin still in the secret drawer of his desk, which of course was the property of his employer. Everyone was ignorant of the coin's being in the drawer and so eventually, after a few generations of furniture movement throughout the family the desk, now in need of refurbishment, was sold to a furniture dealer, one Pierre Beauchamp, who renovated old furniture for resale. It was during the renovation of the secretary desk that the drawer was opened, and the coin discovered. He is clearly seen in Shonakian videos admiring his discovery. Pierre was only too happy to take the coin for himself. It was one of the perquisites of the trade, as people were always hiding things away in their desks and then forgetting about them or dying or whatever.

The year is now +1704 UAY, and Pierre sells the coin to a dealer in Paris, happy at the nice sum he received for it. The coin dealer, a Monsieur Henri Bredotot, places it in a felt-lined cabinet drawer with others of the Ptolemy period, all available for sale. Within the year the coin is sold to another dealer with clients who specialize in these coins. It was duly sold to the wife of a businessman for a birthday present and he had it for a year and a half before losing it. He searched the house and his office but never found it. But his janitor at the office, one Herman Piquot, did find it and he promptly sold it in a local café to the barman, in return for two glasses of vin ordinaire every day for a month.

The barman, who loved to take it out and look at it from time to time, gave it to his mistress, Helen Beaumont, who had it mounted in a brooch fitting. She wore it often, to hold her cloak together at the top, until in +1710 UAY it was snatched while she was walking down a crowded street, tearing her cloak in the process. The thief ran off down an alley and vanished from sight. That thief, wanting to get rid of it quickly, took the coin brooch to a local pawn shop and sold it there. The pawn shop owner, Michel Vigny, had many nice things but he especially liked this coin. He took it out of the brooch and carried it in his watch pocket until he retired in +1720 UAY. As he had no family, he sold everything in his shop to a friend who lived in Switzerland, another pawn shop owner and antiquary dealer. That dealer, Klaus Dengg, was visiting Michel to help him celebrate his retirement and he admired the "good luck" coin Michel showed him. Klaus said he absolutely must have it – how much did he want for it? Michel didn't want to part with it but Klaus was persistent and offered him so much for it he could not say no. It was in this way that the coin departs France for Switzerland. Klaus loaded up everything Michel sold him, and he departed Paris with the collections of several other local dealers as well.

The trip through France by coach and accompanying cargo wagon was uneventful until a wheel fell off his coach, tipping it over, and toppling some heavy chests strapped to the roof into a steep, rocky ravine. The furniture items were safely behind them in the cart but the smaller jewelry and coin items were in the chests on the roof of Klaus' coach. Several of the chests broke on the rocks in the gorge and scattered their contents on the ground, among the rocks and even into the stream at the bottom. Klaus and his workers spent the remainder of that day and the next recovering what they could until exhaustion and bad weather forced them to abandon the hunt, which by then was only finding a coin here and there. The merchant was sorry for the loss of any coins, but he was satisfied that they had made the best of a bad accident. The wheel was repaired while they were searching for the lost items in the gully and so they left the site of the mishap, continuing the trip home. The coin we are following was not recovered during the search and so remained in the ravine. He regretted not putting that special coin he liked in his pocket instead of in the chest but there was nothing to be done about it now.

In +1804 UAY Napoleon's engineers were making improvements to the roads to facilitate the movement of his armies and the site of the earlier mishap was one of the places where work was underway. One of the road engineers, Captain Charles Martine, was at the bottom of the gully near the stream, estimating the work needed to build a retaining wall. He was prying some rocks loose to determine how much soil covered the bedrock when he noticed something shiny in the hole. He dug with his fingers and brushed away some mud to find three silver coins! He was surprised but happy all the same and rooted around there until he determined there were no more to be found. He continued his work and of course told his friends of his discovery that night in their nearby inn. They were happy for him and they talked for days about his find and what he should do with the coins. They also speculated endlessly about how the coins came to be in the gully and how much they might be worth. They would have been surprised to learn that they had been there since the year +1720 UAY! The group enjoyed handling them and talking about them, with nothing much better to do with their rare free time in the evenings and Captain Martine told them all he would never sell the one coin, the big silver one, he prized the most, and proudly showed them again the coin we are following. This is how it was perfectly imaged by Shonakian sensor bots at the bar. Because he favored it so much, he kept that coin separate from the other two, and eventually sold the other two coins to an antiquary dealer in Paris when he returned home. He kept the beautiful tetra drachma with Alexander on the face, and an eagle on the reverse. It is now +1805 UAY and the coin is safely in a wooden box Captain Martine has had since childhood.

He made the box himself, because he loved making things, and though it was not beautiful to anyone else, it was to him. The rusty iron nails holding it together only made him smile at the memory of hammering them in, and hitting his thumb more than once, when just a boy. His father said he used too many nails, but he disagreed. He always felt that anything worth doing was worth over doing. It gave him pride at the thought that he still found uses for his box after all this time. He was also proud of the things he had collected on his army travels which the box held nicely. This box went into his attic and he gradually forgot about it. There was much else to think about with the turmoil caused by the Napoleonic wars swirling around France and the various kingdoms and empires in Europe. His son inherited the family home in +1824 UAY and never thought to look in the attic or in that old box up there. In +1870 UAY the house and its contents passed to a cousin, Joules Nahant, who rummaged through the attic but while he noticed the crude wooden box, did not want to go near it, not with that family of ugly, dark gray spiders who seemed to have made the outside of it their home. Anyway, he thought that at best there might be some old clothes or tools inside it. Surely, he muttered, nothing of value would be put in such a crude container, so did not bother to look inside. The house and its contents stayed in the family until +1910 UAY when the last of the line sold it to a young farmer, Marc Montfort, and his family moved in.

The farmer's oldest son, Pierre, wanted to build himself a room in the attic and so cleared it out. He put everything found there on display in the yard in back of the house and they all eagerly sorted through the odds and ends from the attic. They found a number of things they could use but nothing of particular value, certainly not any unexpected treasure, which the children were very vocal about finding. Eventually one of the children opened the crude box. And there were the "treasures" they wanted! The last box to be opened, crudely made, dirty, unpainted, covered in spider webs, and yet what things were inside! The crudely-made the box was found to be clean on the inside and the contents had all been carefully folded inside a heavy old French officer's uniform coat from maybe the Napoleonic wars, with some military rank insignia, buttons with the Napoleonic Eagle on them, some papers, and a poster from Napoleon's campaign in northern Italy in +1796 UAY. There were two old pistols from the same era, along with cleaning tools and materials and some powder and balls. The boy going through it, while the family and Shonak sensors looked on, took out a small field telescope, dramatically stretched it out, and was amazed at what he could see through it! The last thing to come out of the box, from a bottom corner, up against one of the iron brads, was a large, tarnished silver coin, stuck there by what looked like melted wax from a sealing stick. He pried the coin out and held it up in the bright sunshine of the yard and admired its artistry and handed it to his father. Though tarnished he could see it was silver, and very nicely wrought. He put it in his pocket, thinking to have it cleaned and appraised by a friend of his who collected coins. Within the week he and his friend were admiring the coin and the friend offered him a good bit of money for it. The farmer agreed instantly, and the coin passed to the friend, Armand Vaillancourt, an amateur coin collector, who put the coin in his collection without cleaning it of tarnish or wax or the iron rust from the nail it had been resting on. This coin remained in his possession until after the Great War when he gave it to his son, Hector, who admired it and asked to have it. In their year +1929 UAY the coin is still in Paris, unknown to anyone that it was one of the Thirty Pieces of Silver. It sat in Hector's small, very modest coin collection until the world depression hit and in 1933, and he was forced to sell off most of his possessions, including his coin collection. It was the only way to keep a roof over their heads and food on the family table. The coin thus passed to a German dealer in furniture and other household items and whatever else he could make a profit from.

This German, Helmut Driess, was a Heidelberger living in Trier, a few days by coach to the north on the Moselle River. The coin was a part of the German's inventory until it was purchased, in 1938, along with a dozen other coins of the period, by a French dealer and the coin returned to France, to the city of Metz. Here the coin remained, sold back and forth by dealers, filling out their collections of specialty coins, and it survived WWII untouched by the conflict raging around it. One dealer, Yvres Majeure, took a strong fancy to the coin who decided not to ever sell it and it remained in his collection until his own son and then grandson took over his collections.

The coin was sold again, in +1999 UAY, to an American soldier stationed in Germany. He found the coin during a visit to the famous Metz flea market, a place where over many hectares of buildings and grounds nearly everything can be bought or sold. The coin caught his eye immediately and he was very interested in it and talked at some length with the coin dealer about his collection. Not knowing anything about coins from antiquity he worried about what he considered to be a very low price, too low it seemed, which to him was an indication it was a fake. He did not buy the coin that day but when he researched it later, he learned that the price was in the right range. He then he found out how much is should weigh and what its dimensions should be and two weeks later he returned to the flea market hoping it was still available. The coin dealer was in the same place so easy to find and the American soldier examined the coin, finding it to be the correct size and weight. He noticed the rusty spot on the back of the coin and mentioned that silver does not rust. The dealer explained that this had likely come from a nail head in a box the coin rested in for years. He could not explain the small bit of red wax on the back, but he did say he took care not to clean it lest he disturb the coin's provenance. The dealer went on to explain that these incredibly old coins survived largely because they were kept in hoards, or chests, of gold or silver of a known weight, for centuries. This was how large merchants and lords transferred money amongst themselves rather than count out hundreds of coins every time land or armies were purchased, for example. Satisfied, the American bought the coin and took it to a jeweler in Mannheim, Germany where it was cleaned and mounted in an 18K yellow gold setting. For the next several years he wore it around his neck on a long, heavy gold chain. He retired from the Army in 2000 and settled eventually in Massachusetts. In 2005 he took it to his jeweler in Boston to be set into an 18K gold ring, with the proviso that the coin would not be damaged in the process. He noted with some chagrin that the gold setting cost many times what he paid for the silver coin itself; but considered it absolutely worth the investment.

He had it mounted in a ring so it could be seen, whereas before it had always been invisible under his clothing on the long neck chain. He told his wife and friends that he well knew wearing this ring was risky for the coin because it would inevitably be scratched or gouged with normal wear and tear. As a result, he did not wear it every day, but he did wear it. Once while on vacation in Athens, Greece, where he thought the ring would be appropriate and appreciated, a jewelry shop owner in the Plaka, their ancient market area, scolded him for wearing it at all, telling him it belonged in a museum of Greek heritage. Of course, if either of them even suspected it was one of the Thirty Pieces of Silver there would have been a much different conversation, but such was not the case. As it happened our owner thanked the jeweler for his concern and said that it was a tribute to the coin and its heritage to be worn so that both he and the people around him could enjoy its beauty, wherever he traveled in the world. As noted in the photos, he also wore the ring on a vacation to Australia in +2017 UAY where it was captured in the photo below. He was sitting at a sidewalk café near Victoria Market happily drinking a flat white with his lovely wife, Eleanor. Whenever the coin becomes tarnished, he cleans it by rubbing it with toothpaste with his fingers until silvery-shiny again. The coin's story will continue when this owner leaves the ring with its special coin to his oldest son.

These are two of many bot-accessible pictures of the coin, the last of the "Thirty Pieces of Silver" from more than two thousand years earlier. The first is an insurance policy proof of possession photo and the second is our owner in 2017 on a visit to Melbourne, Australia. It can be seen (as shown) on the hand holding the coffee mug.

Diary Number Nine

Humbot Influencing a Famous Earther – Wolfgang Amadeus Mozart

Faculty Introduction. Some humbots are intentionally provocative. They are constructed, programmed, and dispatched into a location or a social setting specifically to encourage interesting activity for the enjoyment of the Vid-Watch clubs that dispatch them. In this case a Vid-Watch club devoted to classical Earther music of their +eighteenth century UAY, requested a humbot for certain operations in the social circles connected with music composition. Exciting new music was being developed there and then and they wished to stimulate more. Their search for a humbot family in that area of Earth was fruitful. One humbot son of a prosperous humbot mill owner, a master miller in fact, was redirected to work in the musical society there. He quit his job as a miller to do this and became quite influential. This humbot's name was Josef Mysliveček. He was documented as "born" on the 9ᵗʰ of March +1737 UAY in Prague, Czechoslovakia to this long-standing, well respected clandestine humbot family. He and his twin brother both pursued the family mill business until +1762 UAY when Josef was redirected. He suddenly quit the trade to pursue a life of music, much to the "dismay" of his business-oriented family. With family money he was comfortable by the standards of other aspiring musicians and by the year +1771 UAY he was made a member of the Philharmonic Academy of Bologna, Italy. He was a popular member of the music scene in Venice,

Bologna, Naples and Rome, with numerous admirers who helped pay for his "pleasures", all of which were designed to draw out these attributes in the Earthers he was sent to watch and record. He was flamboyantly gregarious, attracting attention within his music circles, and creating for himself a thoroughly "Bohemian" reputation for open sexuality with and towards both men and women. His musical compositions and other works were all designed to maintain his cover as a wealthy and somewhat decadent, affable musician and composer. Shonakian scientists had long before identified the mathematical structure of Earther music and humbot Josef's programming could easily have made him a world famous composer and musician. His assignment, however, was to influence and record, not dominate, the music culture of his time and place. As a musician he was notably gifted at the piano, the violin, and the flute. As a composer he was well known and even acclaimed in his adopted Italy. His greatest achievement in this assignment was his association with the younger composer Wolfgang Amadeus Mozart, one of the most celebrated musicians of all time on Earth and whose reputation and popularity has not only endured over time but has actually improved.

Recognizing the young man's talent, humbot Josef engineered a meeting with Wolfgang's father, Leopold, and then met Wolfgang Amadeus Mozart in Bologna in +1770 UAY. It is the interaction the Josef-humbot had with Wolfgang that forms the essence of this diary. It exemplifies how a humbot can influence the life direction of an Earther, even one of great renown. We leave it to history to determine just how much this interaction directly or indirectly influenced the young Mozart, the Earther in question, but there is no question of the substantial contact that was achieved. Humbot Control wanted the Josef-bot to be credibly human and so was concerned that Josef Mysliveček never married, as so many of his contemporaries did. As a result, Josef did nothing to stop the rumors he spread about various love affairs he had with a variety of women and some hints, in some circles, of liaisons with other men. He was fully functional sexually but of course was a machine and had no innate sexual desires. However, Humbot Control used his supposed sexual excesses to further establish him as a leader of the Bohemian musical subculture, a situation that provided much popular surveillance production for his Vid-Watch club. Joseph "died" in Rome in +1781 UAY, reportedly of syphilis, which is a sexually transmitted disease. He was a machine incapable of contracting a disease but this story was created to maintain his cover as an Earther human. Prior to his "death" he underwent a few dramatic disease-related surgeries, by Shonak's bot maintenance facility, that disfigured him, showed him losing weight, losing healthy coloring, etc., all of which served to cement his reputation as one of the music scene's "talented bad boys". His complete files are available for later database search if desired, but this diary is not about Josef, but rather about the potential for bots to influence Earthers using WA Mozart as an example.

Diary. In +1770 UAY the thirty-three year old humbot Josef Mysliveček met fourteen-year-old Wolfgang Amadeus Mozart in Bologna, Italy and determined immediately that the boy was a talent who would make a good surveillance and influence target. In pursuit of this goal he remained close to the Mozart family for eight years, after which he engineered a falling out with them to pursue other targets for Vid-Watch exploitation. The Vid-Watchers controlling Josef felt he was spending too much time with Mozart so they engineered a broken promise over a contract for Wolfgang in Naples. This caused a permanent rift between them but in the eight years of their close friendship, our bot had considerable contact with and influence over the younger Mozart. Their early days of friendship enamored Wolfgang for his new friend and they were seen in frequent collaboration over bits and pieces of music. Music theory fascinated Mozart and of course our bot knew every aspect the science and technique of it so their conversations and musings at the piano keyboard make great watching. Care was taken to keep Josef from appearing smarter than Mozart while still sharing bits and pieces of unique music composition and instrumentation. Josef recorded it all as Mozart dissected and resected pieces each of them wrote, as well as borrowing liberally from the compositions of others.

Similarities in Josef's musical style with the earlier works of Mozart are often noted by Earther music scholars. Additionally, Mozart used musical elements from various of Josef's compositions to help fashion a variety of operatic and symphonic concertos.

To expand his sphere of influence, Humbot Control encouraged Josef to become a not-so-secret Freemason, and a member of the more secret Illuminati. This was done to achieve better coverage of these specific intellectuals at such an important time in their history.

Earthers in that part of the world were discarding the shackles of religious dogma and the status quo and numerous Vid-Watch clubs wanted to see it happen. It was Josef, then, who sowed the seeds for Mozart's future with the Masonic brotherhood. Joseph even self-chartered his own Masonic Lodge in Venice in order to attract the cream of the local gentlemen passionately following the Enlightenment philosophy and writing of their heroes, Rousseau, Voltaire, Kant, and Locke.

The Vid-Watch masters of the humbot Joseph wanted to follow the Earthers who were adopting this new way of thinking, freed from so much social and church dogma, to see where it would lead them. Joseph's "secret" Lodge was named the Three Kings, or Trium Regum, in Latin. The vid record of this Lodge in Venice is available after you receive your red dots but in this context, it was a springboard for Joseph to help sow the seeds of the Enlightenment wherever he traveled and his bona fides as Master of the Trium Regum Lodge gave him entre to the precise circles his Vid-Watch club desired. When Joseph met and cultivated his friendship with Mozart he was able to captivate Mozart's attention with a marriage of Enlightenment ideals with his passionate style of music composition. Interestingly, the bot Joseph also influenced the character of the broader community of Italian Freemasons, which was loosely confederated in the late 18th century but whose Grand Lodge was not formally established until 1805 UAY. Freemasonry today enjoys a great many followers in Vid-Watch clubs around the whole of Shonak, and like the rest of the planet's subcultures, it is different in every different country.

Mozart mentions Freemasonry often in his letters and conversations, but he did not join a lodge until 1784, three years after Josef's "death". Mozart's Masonic membership significantly influenced his composition which can be seen in his final seven years of composing. It also influenced his choice of friends and companions which further influenced his life and music. Earther scholars of music history have noted hints of Masonic ritual in a variety of his works. These are all available to Earthers and Shonakians interested in following this up. What the Earthers don't have, however, are the many compositions of Mozart that were not always even written down, and some that were destroyed as he lit fires with the papers or used them as notes to his wife and family and friends. Literally hundreds of Mozart's works are lost to Earther history but not to Shonakian databases. There is no way to share them with Earthers without letting them know just how extensive and long-standing our surveillance operation is and has been on Earth. A Mozart composition he played only once, merely to amuse himself or family or friends, never written down, would be gone forever once the final note died out. We have it all recorded but cannot let them know. Perhaps we can "release" these things through Helen Manners historical research company as speculative pieces based on scraps and fragments of his works that have survived.

Diary Number Ten

Information Integrity – How Shonak Helped Earth Overcome their Assault on Truth

Faculty Introduction. Another fundamental difference between Shonak and Earth is the integrity of information available to the public. On Shonak, there has never been an intentional falsification or manipulation of information, very likely because there has never been any reason to falsify anything. What would be gained? And much, we all know, would be lost, most importantly our trust in each other and for any and all information. We understand that our team of teams cannot achieve its missions when false information forms the basis of any decision.

As a false piece of information enters the data stream it will have some impact on other pieces of information, help inform subsequent decisions, and will be layered over with other pieces of information which over time renders it virtually impossible to trace, track, or pin down as the cause of some problem or miscalculation. And that is with a single erroneous bit of information. Imagine, then, how Earth copes with a reality where some large percentage of information in their global data steam is either totally false, intentionally misleading, or incomplete. Everything based on it will therefore be in some way false, misleading or incomplete.

And as can be seen on Earth time and time again, false information has a way of propagating itself and burying itself into the factors of decisions far beyond what may have been intended. The term they use is "unintended long-term consequences" and there are so many examples of it. They pay for this every day on Earth, since the "truth" is elusive, and all information is suspect as a result. This causes exponentially expanding indecisiveness because as information flows from person to person over time it is the basis upon which so many things can and do result. There are on Earth, unlike on Shonak, so many reasons the natives find to lie and to pass bad information along to others so the solution to this problem eluded them for millennia. Even before information on Earth was automated lying about everything, large or small, was a part of life and people knew they must accept things cautiously. Essentially, they knew to suspect everything they read or heard. But at the beginning of publishing and the beginning of their Internet honesty was prevalent and there was integrity and restraint in the system. People tended to trust the written word placed in public forums like government publications, books, magazines, newspapers and radio and television. The following diary shows how we helped them improve their respect for the truth.

Diary. Earther behavior was something we loved to observe but when they were able to reduce information to automation they placed it into globally available formats. Eventually the high percentage of false, misleading, or incomplete data became a problem, even for us here on Shonak. We were not accustomed to dealing with false information and while we were able to spot it immediately it became so prolific the very nature of our Earther watching changed as it was overwhelmed by it. In the late + twentieth century UAY, their version of our Comm was called the Internet and it spanned the globe in a short number of years. Since everything they do has a money angle, this led to the commercialization of information which in turn led to making information more attractive in order to make it more popular. Popularity led things to be more profitable and to continue that trend the thinking was everything must appeal to audiences in a positive way. This led to content manipulation designed to maximize the number of people who chose to watch, promote, purchase, use, buy again, continuously and on a global scale. This thinking became politicized so that content was designed to favor one position over another, one candidate over another, regardless of truth on any particular topic. Eventually people ended up believing what they wanted to believe since nobody knew what the real truth was.

Professional politicians were at the vanguard of the transformation from truth to fiction but the many other spokespersons for the various ideologies in vogue at the time also wreaked havoc on the truth. It became common to give only partial truths or outright lies in order to attract attention and the money that came with that by selling space and airtime to advertisers. In addition to misinformation within a nation there was misinformation between and among nations designed to further national agendas at the expense of others. Battlefield dominance remained a sporadic problem, but information dominance became a much less expensive approach and one that a single individual could exploit as easily as an army or a country. Malicious software designed to inject faulty information or damage computer function or pollute information databases was common and damaging to public trust and business success. We see from analysis of the data here on Shonak that almost every negative behavior on Earth can at some point be traced to a false or misleading piece of information. They even knew this and professed not to care.

This was an unhappy situation for Shonakian Vid-Watchers because we found intentional information pollution to be uninteresting and wrong so we determined to help them fix it. In their mid-plus twenty-first century UAY we insinuated specifically prepared humbots into positions of influence in order to begin the process of helping them fix it themselves. We directed our humbots in government staff positions to draft legislation in multiple influential countries for use when various information network disasters happened. At that time they could get the attention of lawmakers and policy makers and make their proposals. National laws were woven into international treaties and later into world government law to protect Earth, and our Vid-Watchers from the pitfalls of information pollution.

Eventually, intentional disinformation and network and data intrusions, information manipulation, identity theft and false logins were made illegal. Punishment was severe and often swift. Once CRIMISLE was established and crimes of all types including information crimes were discovered with the aid of Shonakian technology, there was a visible decline in malicious behavior online.

Earth also became much more practical in their approach to how data was created, stored, and moved about on their worldwide information networks. With our help, again using our humbot "experts" in positions of influence, Earthers began to realize the Internet was not some mythically holy place untouchable by governments; a fantasy hoped for by many but unfortunately never achieved. They finally saw it for what it really was, just another public utility like water, sewer, power and they regulated it accordingly.

And with our behind the scenes advice and assistance, their approach to fixing things was systematic. To begin with, all schools taught various levels of proper internet behavior. This education was seen in the same light as learning to drive a vehicle on public roads. In order to log onto the Internet they must first complete a mandatory curriculum which taught them what they needed to know about confidentiality, integrity, and availability of information and devices, whether on wired or wireless connections. Data privacy, copyright protection, personal information security, courtesy, and the laws were all taught, and tests passed in order for the students to demonstrate they had learned the fundamentals to join the Internet safely and securely. When granted access students were given a biometrically based identification, using their iris, a unique password, and status in life. If they were a student they had certain access and if a nuclear engineer they were given another. This ensured that their access was commensurate with their needs, according to their age, position, and for minors, parental permission. Adults were also required to take this training and education and pass the same tests, if they had not already done so through school or work or on their job. They also were given an online ID based on their iris, and all the rest. In this way all connections to the Internet followed a standard which recognized that user identification must be a fundamental part of each connection. Anonymous access disappeared. Speed and reliability had been the only two information network mandates and these were business standards, not government standards. Information Assurance, which blends hardware, software, firmware, training and education with information integrity became the "third leg of the milk stool" as contemporary comment noted, after speed and reliability. This went a long way in ending the naïve charade that the Internet was (or should be) an apolitical, global zone of unlimited freedom of expression. That mentality enabled terrorists to recruit people on a global scale and show their grisly beheadings to a global audience. With the new laws and procedures a more useful era for information flow was ushered in with no less control of the Internet borders than for any other print or visual media. Restrictions were enforceable. All access was logged and available for reconstruction when the needs arose, as for some legal proceeding. There was also a shift from an extra-national entity controlling the Internet to one of national and then world government control. In the end all nations established their own rules which effectively ended the notion of an unregulated Internet without borders.

Fundamental to these changes was the end of anonymous presence. Only people who had been issued a government online ID, based on their iris, password, and status could access any part of the internet, with verified special status providing the ability to achieve special access. This was unlike in the first decades of the Internet where anyone could log on with any identity they chose and people who intended to commit crimes on the internet or otherwise misbehave, they could do so with little thought of being caught. That single improvement ended the majority of common crime and misbehavior. It did not stop all cybercrime but it went a long way in keeping honest people honest. Another change ended insecure/insufficiently tested software applications and faulty hardware production and installation. All vendors of hardware, firmware, and software were both criminally and civilly liable for what they produced and how it was installed. If there was faulty code, embedded malware, or unforeseen complications with other applications or operating systems they were held to task and faced CRIMISLE for intentional violations. This also resulted in a great reduction of Internet problems. Data privacy was also mandated so when computers of other Internet devices communicated to their manufacturers it could only be to improve products and services, and no longer to sell private information or usage data. Another fundamental change was the end the "one size fits all" Internet. The various categories of information flowing over the Internet were separated into different networks of a single purpose. Financial data was passed on the financial network, which required a separate, status-based biometric logon which was appropriately logged in that network's access servers. This was also true for medical information, entertainment, news, government, critical infrastructure, religion, electronic mail, shopping, social media, and the like. There was even a separate network for completely unregulated information for those people who wanted no controls but it was, like other networks, completely separate with no connections to the other portions of the global or national Internet.

Finally, all Internet connections by the machinery that controlled critical infrastructure was placed on its own secure network and only accessible by cleared people whose job it was to work on those systems.

Diary Number Eleven

Influencing Earther Myths and Legends

Faculty Introduction: Earthers created myths and legends to explain natural phenomena they had no science to understand. Things like the sun and the moon mystified them and so they developed supernatural explanations for them as well as the four seasons, thunder and lightning, and so on. As their science developed their myths and legends retreated before the assault of reason and proof. What they once believed they now consider entertaining fiction. Up to a point. One of the aspects of Earther natures is the fact that certain beliefs do not fall back or fade away when confronted by rational thought or facts. This diary will provide you with insights you will need when viewing their religious and spiritual behavior.

Diary. In the year -723 UAY, in a mountain village near Aeolis city, near the eastern shore of their Inland Sea, an unplanned bot-sighting took place. A Shonakian Orange and two humbots were accidentally seen by a Earther shepherd boy. They duly noted and logged the incident for Plus-Five Base. These humbots, and the phase suit worn by the Orange, were early versions without the threat detection sensors in later versions which would have prevented this sighting by the boy. Humbots were a relatively new development and these two were being fielded to provide better Vid-Watch coverage of the growing population in the region. The Eldest of the fielding team, a young Orange, was new to Plus-Five but had always been an avid vid-watcher and was greatly enamored of the world and its people. The Orange, in his phase suit, was checking the required behavior of the latest generation humbots he was fielding and asked them to wrestle each other for strength and dexterity function. Since the bots were of Plus-Five native materials they were naturally stable at this vibration and looked perfectly human.

The shepherd boy was innocently rounding up his family's flock for the daily journey back to their pen when he topped a rise and saw the wrestling match. He saw two naked men wrestling each other, without much energy, he thought, and some sort of small, skinny shimmering monster watching them! This "monster" was the Orange who was phasing in and out of the scene and appeared like an apparition until he fully phased in to Plus-Five and was stable there – but the shimmering of his phase suit was impossible to hide. The Orange had been using anti-grav and was two or three short measures off the ground, flying around so he could maintain the best views of his bots who were supposed to be wrestling as if they were human. He would not be comfortable fielding them until they could be convincing in every conceivable Earther situation. He had seen them eat and drink, converse in several local languages, dress accordingly and their construction was true to the appearance of the people in this area. Wrestling was the last item on his checklist. He noted that they broke out into a sweat appropriately and he could see that their internal water supply was reduced accordingly. Their eyes remained moist and one of the men spat at the other, who spat back, showing that they were able to do what Earthers expected of them. His sensors told him their body temperature had risen appropriately to the intensity of their workout. That completed his checklist. Then the lamb our shepherd boy was chasing bleated, they looked around and saw the boy, and saw that he had seen them. In the blink of an eye all three suddenly disappeared! They had phased away from Plus-Five and gained altitude before half-phasing back in to watch the boy's reaction. They saw him stop dead in his tracks and stare at the place they had been, mouth open, totally mystified. They saw him staring at the place where the ground was disturbed by their wrestling test but he was looking around rapidly to see where they went! He looked up, then, and saw them high, like birds, but shimmering and see-through. What manner of things were they? He looked at them one more time, he looked again at the grass where the wrestlers were, and they saw him suddenly break into a run, down the mountain. They could see he had forgotten all about his sheep and was running back to his village. No doubt he would tell people there what he had seen. The Orange directed all the mobile surveillance sensors in the area to concentrate on the boy and his run to the village, and what he did when he got there, in order to capture the totality of their reaction. They were able to see the boy run into the village and find his father, who was chopping wood for the family hearth.

His father listened to his tale, which was blurted out quickly, but their sensors captured it all. At first the father appeared to be listening patiently but then became agitated and stood up from the stump was sitting on and asked his son somewhat angrily and very concerned, "And where is our flock while all this is going on? Who is watching them now? Are they feeding the wolves somewhere up there?" The boy stopped – eyes wide – suddenly remembering his family's flock, and that he was responsible for it, and they noted that he immediately ran away, back up the mountain, to gather the sheep. He got back late but he returned with them all.

After he ate his cold supper the boy told his tale again, this time to the whole family, gathered in the common room by the fire. An array of tiny mobile sensors was collecting it all. His two brothers were wide eyed with wonder and were clearly impressed and believing every word. His father said he was skeptical but admitted that the details in his story made it almost believable. His mother asked him where he got so vivid an imagination and said she did not believe a word. His sister said he had seen magic. And he told them he didn't know exactly what he saw, or what he thought of it. It seemed so unreal, he said, that maybe he would have a better idea in the morning, and wandered over to his sleeping pallet.

Humbot Control at Plus-Five Base was also reviewing the incident. The Eldest of Control was considering next steps in consultation with his Elder, the Eldest of Plus-Five Base. What he did do immediately was to deploy even more sensors of all types in and around the village to catch gossip and gauge the impression made by the boy's story. They noted that it had made the rounds of the village in less than a Planetary Rotation. In fact, by sundown of the following day, the men of the village, knowing the boy to be an honest lad, decided to trek up to the spot where he had witnessed the wrestlers and their sudden disappearance. They were not sure what to think of the alleged "monster" the boy claimed he also saw. Their real purpose was fear of the unknown and they wanted desperately to understand what kind of new threat might now be present around them. They wanted, they kept saying, to find it and then kill it. The boy led them all to the precise location of the incident and of course the ground was back to normal and nothing was to be seen except the now peaceful site of dirt and sparse grass and boulders with a nice view of their valley below and the ocean in the far distance. Bot Control, using an eagle-bot to witness and follow the congregation of village men, decided to see what would happen if they were indeed seen by humans there. Since this was an isolated village, of no great importance, it was felt that any stories they would tell would be ignored or dismissed as the ramblings of backwards, uneducated villagers. Humbot Control agreed it was the right thing to do.

The Orange who had been seen the day before flew back to the mountain by the village, half-phased away from Plus-Five, then phased back in when he arrived, hovering about ten feet off the ground, just near enough to the men so they could clearly see him. The men gasped, and cowered, and cried out, and one of them grabbed a rock and threw it at the Orange, who quickly dodged away from it. He held up his hands in a gesture of peace and spoke to them in their own language. He said he was no threat to them and meant them no harm. He said he only wanted to talk. After a pause, one of the men walked nearer to him, looked directly up at him and asked, "What manner of creature are you, then, to come here and fly like a bird, and make the air around you shimmer like a rock on a hot day?" The Orange replied that he was from another world. He did not want to go into an explanation of Shonak to these people, so he simply said he was from a world of gods, who enjoyed watching the people here and meant them no harm. He asked them if they would be willing to help his family of gods with a problem they were having. The men all looked at one another and muttered to themselves and this went on for a while until their spokesman, the shepherd boy's father, asked what they could to do help. The Orange, thinking quickly, said he would return the following day with the answer, and then phased out and disappeared. The men were startled by his sudden departure and jumped back, with a few inadvertent cries of alarm. Several stones were thrown at the place in the air where the "monster" had been but they just sailed up and then down, hitting nothing. The men stood around a bit for what seemed like too long then as one, filed back down the sheep trail to their village, wondering what surprises were in store for them on the following day. Static sensors along the way and various animal sensors picked up little in the way of useful information. Mostly they were sobered by the experience which was so far outside anything they could imagine it quieted them all down. None of them, they were sure, would ever be quite the same again. The Orange flew back to Plus-Five Base for consultation with his Elders.

Hestor, the boy's father, asked the men of the village to stay close to home the next day. He did not want to trek back up the mountain and said that if this were a god he would surely know they were in the village. There was some grumbling about that but none of them wanted to make the return trip back up there, either, and they all had work to do in the village. It took all their efforts to prepare for winter and they needed every day to get all that done. Hestor gathered the villages elders to the center of their little village and they did not wait long. The Orange phased in to their vibration almost immediately and welcomed them. What women and children that were about quickly scampered into their homes to hide and the men, though nervous, looked up at the Orange who noticed they were all armed with farm tools and there was one sword, and several spears. He thanked them for agreeing to hear his request and once again assured them he was no threat to them. He added that they need not have brought weapons. Hestor said, "That is for us to determine, monster." He added, "Yesterday, you said you wanted our help. We are here to find out what that might be and what we will receive for it in return." To this the Orange replied, "My people wish to know more about your people. It's that simple. We would like to know how you think about certain things, us for example, and in return for your help we can provide assurance of a better harvest, more food for your tables, better ways to extract metal from rock, and better care for the sick and injured. In short, we provide you with an easier life in return for some information from you." The men were stunned. They were silent for a time, thinking about what they just heard and what it meant for their village. They began to speak to one another and got more and more excited. One of them raised his voice, as if the Orange were a long way away, and asked, "What about money, are you going to pay us for our help in addition to these other things?" The Orange, from a cashless society and so not thinking about money, replied, "Yes, of course we will pay you any way you want. Coin or gold or silver, as you choose." The men all erupted with joy! The Orange knew he had just learned a valuable lesson about Earthers; money speaks louder than anything else. The Orange told them that he would appear in their village the next day to begin discussions with all of them, the men, women, and children. They asked for money up front and the Orange, unprepared with any payment, told them they would have to wait till the morning. Then he asked what they were expecting and after some consultation, said, "One Stater as we have many people in our village." The Orange agreed, not that he had a clue as to what might be right and proper, and phased away from them, and disappeared.

Back at Plus-Five base the Orange levied the task of producing the requested real Electrum, but counterfeit coinage, noting these were the earliest coins anywhere they had seen on Plus-Five. The Lydians who made them used a natural pale yellow combination of gold and silver found in their mountains, which they called electrum, and succeeded in regularizing commerce as a result. The concept caught on as everyone understood the advantages of small, portable but valuable metals of a known weight being used for payment for goods and services. Plus-Five base made a request to Grand Team Science and Technology and GT Manufacturing to come up with the two hundred and twenty-one Stater for the following morning's delivery.

The Orange, and Plus-Five Base were about to learn their own valuable lesson about the manipulative side human nature, quite aside from their desire to test out humbot performance and acceptance with the natives. That lesson involved both Earther greed and the inherent goodness of Shonakians, as well as the Earther desire to control, so integral to the humans living on the knife edge of subsistence. One bad harvest, one drought, one severe hailstorm, one epidemic, and their village could be devastated and die out. This is what made them get up before the sun and go to bed long after it was gone. So, suddenly, the village is offered the chance to lift themselves out of the grind of subsistence poverty, and the source of this elevation is some shimmering monster calling itself a "god" who wants their help, and is willing to pay for it!

The next morning, the Orange again appeared in the most central area amongst their hovels and the people who were out and about stopped everything to stare at this sudden apparition. The men had told the women they were to receive a strange "visitor" the next day, with money for them, and the woman dismissed that with a laugh. But now, here it was, hovering about head height, not saying anything, but looking around itself with something of the wonder that they had on their own faces, looking at him. He said, to no one in particular, "I am Orange Nic, and I am here to seek your help in return for such things as were requested by the men of the village last evening." The men were starting to trickle into the square, or central plaza of the village, and Hestor put his hands on his hips and asked where their money was. Immediately a pile of coins appeared below the orange, in a basket, and Hestor rushed to pick it up, finding that it was extremely heavy, almost too heavy for the basket to hold. The Orange said calmly that this was one Stater for all 221 people in the village, regardless of age. Hestor was shocked. He had thought they would receive one stater only, which would feed a family for a month. Instead this apparition had given them one stater for each person in the village! The gods must be rich beyond all imagining. This was wealth they could not have imagined – none of them had actually ever seen a single stater. He told them all to step back, he would dole them out to the men of the families, according to their number. He asked that the men form a line and come to him, with the names of each member of their household. This line was formed quickly and each man said the names of each of them, including himself, and Hestor placed one Stater in his palm for each name. And so it went until all the coins were doled out except his, and he held out his own left hand and put a coin in it after saying all their names. The count was perfect, and he wondered how the god calling himself Orange Nic had known that?

Orange Nic was pleased at their reaction to the payment. What he did not know was the value of a Stater in those days. One of those coins was pay for a soldier for one whole moon cycle. He had just given the village a treasure beyond their wildest dreams, and he had in fact increased the Lydian money supply by 221 Stater! Of course that meant nothing to him since he had never calculated money or wealth or even commerce before. When the counting was done, Nic asked Hestor if he was satisfied. Hestor did not answer immediately. He was beyond satisfied but he wanted to see how far he could push this little monster in terms of money and other things. He told Nic, "You have fulfilled your bargain with the money, and we will fulfill ours in due course. First, however, there were other things you promised us, like better tools, better ways to make them, better harvests, and things like that. When will all that happen?" He paused, and emboldened by the passive features on Nic, said, and of course we will need more money, as well. Orange Nic did not think any of that was out of the question and nodded his assent. Hestor was very happy as were the rest of the villagers, and he could see the beginning of squabbles between men and their wives, and the wives against each other, no doubt over the distribution of their newfound wealth. One woman was yelling at another, Hestor could see it was the mother with the largest number of children, who was suddenly the richest woman in the village. The woman with only one child was telling the other that she should give her some of her coins to make up for her three still-borns and the woman with the large family laughed at her and said these coins were for the physical pain and hard work in caring for her large family. Then she put her hands on her hips, drew herself up to her full height, and asked the other woman if she would come work for her a few days a week to help her care for all those children. The other woman said she would rather have her fingernails pulled out and stomped away, shouting, to no one in particular, that the gods were playing favorites. This was hugely instructive to the Shonakian vie-watcherss, who followed this exchange with great interest. One remarked that they were watching two Earther women, suddenly with more money than they had ever seen, and yet they found reasons for anger and unhappiness. Earthers, he sighed, were a strange lot, unpredictable and incomprehensible! Another Shonakian, one of the Plus-Five Base students of Earther monetary systems, noted that the staters in their possession were too large a denomination to actually use. One of those coins might buy a thousand loaves of bread, and the baker would not have the ability to give them that much bread or make the correct change. The coins represented, if you will, too much wealth in a single coin.

Orange Nic, still above them in the plaza, hearing all this on his comm links, asked them to listen to what his people were expecting from the village in return for the coins and other things. They stopped talking then and paid close attention. Orange Nic said, "My people are eager to know what you think about us gods, now we are here amongst you. We have the ability to do many wonderful things. We can be seen in different guises, we can fly, we can appear and disappear at will. We can make all manner of wonderful things and we can achieve nearly everything we put our minds to. We plan on doing these things so you can see them and then we want your honest responses to our displays of our powers." One of the women in the square, listening intently, laughed out loud, and for quite some time. Her laugh was infectious, and others joined in, as did some of the men. Orange Nic realized that he had been true to the Shonakian method of going straight to the point. He knew, then, he needed to gently move into those displays of magical power and not just get right to it. The woman who began the laughter stopped and got a serious look on her face and asked Nic, "I am the baker's wife and I want a better flour from the mill so I can make better bread, like the bread we have seen in Aeolis." Nic told her he would see to it, and quick-linked the request in comms to his S&T team at Plus-Five Base. He told her he would provide more efficient grinding stones to make a finer flour, one that would react better to the baking process and create bigger, tastier loaves. They beamed at that.

The shepherd boy, Helios, asked it they could explain things like the sun and the moon and the stars at night, and lightening, and thunder, and rain! Orange Nic smiled and said he would be happy to! His father, Hestor, chimed in with his thanks and then asked that in future they be paid in half, third, and sixth portions of Staters, and (he thought he might be pushing his luck a bit here) could that be provided every day they were asked to help? The Orange naively agreed, proving to the villagers that the gods truly had no sense whatsoever for money or the value of work!

Over the next S-Rot Orange Nic and his team worked with the village to give them more advanced ways of making things, growing things, tending to things, and tools for making things. Their payments grew rapidly until one day Hestor told the Orange to stop paying them with coin. He explained to Orange Nic that they had enough money now, and that they preferred to concentrate on other things like tools and clothing and better designs for things. Orange Nic agreed and was pleased that Hestor felt comfortable enough with him to speak freely. In fact, the village was so rich they decided to move to Ephesus and live there, going into business for themselves and establishing themselves as people of means. Their money could actually be used there and the men actually pooled a great deal of their wealth in order to set themselves up in business, which they did. They continued to prosper and did, indeed, live fruitful, comfortable lives.

While still in the village, Eldest, Plus-Five Base was unsure his Orange was doing the right thing but was content for the moment to watch and see what came of it. He did caution the Orange to refrain from using scientific terms these people would not understand so Orange Nic determined to dumb down his explanations and use metaphoric dialogue instead. So instead of the earth revolving around the sun, which they would never understand, he determined that the sun would be a god, in a golden chariot, moving across the sky to light the day so people could see to work. At night, the moon would be a goddess who lit the night gently so people could sleep. The stars in the sky were many, many gods looking down on them all to observe their activities.

The Orange decided to bring some order to their world along with the money and tools and technology they were receiving. He thought it best if he gave their "gods" some structure, akin to their own family structures, complete with names and various attributes and position in the "family". So he told them of Zeus, the father of all the gods and therefore their king. He was the one who determined their overall fate in life, along with such things the people don't understand like the weather. His wife was Hera, the queen, ruler of women and marriage. Aphrodite gave them beauty and love. Apollo provided the gift of prophesy, poetry, knowledge and music. Ares was the god of war, Artemis was the goddess of the hunt, their flocks and the birthing of their animals and families. Athena was their goddess of wisdom and protection. Demeter was their goddess of the harvest. Naturally they needed a god of wine and pleasure so he gave them Dionysus. Their smith and artisans were given Hephaestus the god of fire, metalworking and sculpture. Hermes was their god of travel, hospitality and trade and was Zeus's personal messenger. Then there was Poseidon, the god of the sea, Hades, the god of the underworld, Hestia, goddess of home and family, and Eros, god of sex and helper for Aphrodite. These attributes were given him by the research team at Plus-Five Base, matching gods to the things Earthers involved themselves in and felt the most passionate about.

Orange Nic took an interest in the boy, Helios, also known in the village as Hesiod, and spent time with him trying to make at least one villager knowledgeable of more advanced concepts, to see how those might filter out from him to others in the village or the region. This work with Hesiod continued in parallel with the focus group activity Orange Nic and his team were doing. The boy's keen interest in what the Orange was telling him was apparent although it was hard to determine if he was really understanding the universe as described to him. This boy, living in early Earther civilization, had no knowledge of astronomy, or physics, or even that he was on a round planet, revolving on an axis, circling the sun while trapped by its gravitational pull. What the Orange could not know was what he was thinking, or the dreams Hesiod was having, and would continue to have all his life. Unless he confided in someone out loud it could not be collected. Shonakian technology was good but not so good as to read Earther minds – or Shonakian minds either! And dreaming is something Shonakians don't think about since Shonakians never dream. In fact, Shonakians only know about dreams from the descriptions of them Earthers enjoy sharing with others. From what Hesiod tells his friends and family of his dreams clearly indicate a marriage of oral tradition, dreams, and Shonak's attempts to educate him. The Orange was somewhat surprised, therefore, when the boy began to talk about a creation story, the universe's journey from the chaos of nothing which was actually everything, but without form. It was Zeus who brought order to it all and who created their world, people, animals, birds, and everything else while his family of gods watched from their mountain top home. The Orange and his team were able to watch, over the following S-Rots, how Hesiod gave birth to the pantheon of gods and goddesses and connected them to human people. His stories gave them life which the Orange had failed to do. The team on Plus-Five Base followed the development of these myths and legends over the next many centuries, noting how other writers developed their own stories and dramas from these earlier ideas. These flowed from the Greeks to the Romans and to the Norse and the Arabs and Christians into India and Africa to form a complex tapestry of various gods and goddesses to explain physical phenomena without any science to help them. Out of necessity for answers to the unexplainable they turned to magic in the form of gods and goddesses, and later angels and demons and then just stories to frighten or calm children or even adults seeking some comfort amid the chaos of life on the violence-prone planet Shonak knew as Plus-Five, and what the natives came to call Earth. The shimmering aura of Orange Nic's phase suit even managed to be represented in art, with a nimbus of halo appearing above the head of various people and gods of holy virtue!

Diary Number Twelve

In Search of The Soul

Faculty Introduction: For all Shonak's scientific and technical expertise, coupled with our great intelligence, there are aspects of Plus-Five we can only speculate about. This is because certain things Earthers do or take for granted or say they understand or have faith in fall outside the realm of hard science. To be scientific a thing must allow for repeated testing under the same conditions with the same result. The issues we will discuss in this lesson are things for which Shonakians have no history and in fact have no physical substance and therefore no science. The Diary presented here gives you, our students, both the Shonak and the Earther perspective on this admittedly non-scientific issue. As you continue to watch Earthers over your long lives you will form your own opinions. These will likely change over time as you receive more information useful to making your own judgments about these things.

Diary from the Shonak Perspective. On Shonak we have no equivalents for paranormal or religious or spiritual thoughts or behavior. Our great thinkers have determined that this may be due to our inherently slow vibration but it is something we can't reduce to the rigors of scientific testing. The only reason for their conclusion about resonance being the determining factor is not based on scientific inquiry but rather on a comparison between Shonakians and Earthers. Shonakians do not have any history with paranormal or spiritual or religious thoughts or impressions. Our extensive surveillance of Earther behavior clearly indicates that virtually every Earther experiences some form of all these behaviors. Shonakians don't even dream but every Earther does, or claims to. Shonak expended great resources trying to find out if there was a Plus-Six vibration and lost three phase ships sent to find it. If it is true that Plus-Six is at a non-physical vibration and if it is correct that Earthers living so close to it are able to cross over in their minds, if not their bodies, then the diary which follows will make more sense to you. You are of course free to believe what you will about all of this. You will also learn here what OE has determined is the answer. It must be stated that when Shonakians lived for so many years at Plus-Five Base their "closeness" to the mythical Plus-Six did not cause any of them to dream or experience anything approaching paranormal incidents. This was because they were kept at Prime in their Zone of Influence and so were in essence still living on Shonak. The only Shonakian to attempt any "connection" with Plus-Six was our venerated former Emerald Bon. When he was a Gold and Eldest of Plus-Five Base he had a hole cut into the top of his phase suit so the top of his head was actually exposed to Plus-Five's vibration. He could only manage that for a short time and he did report some connection with "impressions of thought". This led to other areas of inquiry which you can read about on your own. My message to you students now is this: There are forces at work on Plus-Five about which we have little to no understanding and they manifest themselves daily, as our surveillance bots consistently show.

One of the things about Earthers which fascinates and frustrates us the most is what they would call the "supernatural" or "spiritual" aspects of their lives. Perhaps because we here at Prime do not and cannot experience it, and because we seek and find rational, science-based explanations for everything, our intense curiosity and desire to understand this more fully is understandable, in spite of its non-scientific nature. It is well known and accepted on Shonak that many, if not most Earthers claim to possess an alien presence which they call a "soul". This is not a physical presence and therefore cannot be seen under autopsy or x-ray or interrogation. From the Shonakian scientific point of view it does not exist and yet it persists in the minds and actions of most if not all Earthers. So what is it, then? Shonak has explored and provided an answer to this question but Emerald Bon modified the decision of a previous OE by stating it will be up to future generations of Shonakians to uncover the truth.

Stated simply, many Earthers believe they have a soul and that this soul does not die when their body dies. The truth of this is actually better known on Shonak since we have the unemotional and therefore correct view, while on Earth there is almost universal disagreement as to every aspect of this belief. With hundreds of often overlapping, often conflicting or contrary views on the subject all over their planet Earthers are left to judge for themselves or listen to religious explanations they prefer. Often they defer to religion and religious leaders to supply them with the "correct" way to think of these things, e.g. supreme beings and the soul. In this sense Earthers and Shonakians are alike in that we also defer to a higher authority, our OE, since there can be no scientific explanation.

Our extensive surveillance of Plus-Five has enabled us to review every culture in detail including all religious cultures, across the entire planet. We capture most words and most deeds and when we have questions, we place appropriately dressed humbots among them, to ask questions, in their own languages, to help clarify some of these thoughts and actions. While there is a basic similarity among many of the religious beliefs and practices, the diversity they represent is huge. The two thing they have in common is belief in one or more gods and goddesses and in the ability to reach out to them through prayer and/or some sort of offering. A few of their belief systems have only one supreme being but these are in the minority. We have catalogued just over sixteen thousand different interpretations and are still looking for more which are sufficiently different to list them separately. Not surprisingly, the violent nature of these people is reflected in their religious rites and beliefs. Historically, animal and human sacrifice were common but this has diminished over time. Prayer is a common practice among many cultures on Earth. Most Earthers believe that if they please their gods in some way their wishes will be granted. It may be a wish for a better harvest, healthy babies, long life, more wealth and power, victory in battle, better weather, or healing some sort of sickness or deformity. Curiously, enemies each pray that they will succeed and their opponents will fail, putting their gods in competition with each other. When questioned on this point they each claim that their gods are more powerful, more understanding, more generous, more victorious than the gods of their enemies. Both sides make these claims which to us, at least, shows how superficial, self-serving, and inherently wrong the whole concept is. Favoritism by their gods is assumed, and is supplemented by ritual sacrifice, professed loyalty, and other offerings, not to mention faith, which Earthers seem to have in abundance regardless of the outcomes.

The issue of souls is common among them too but the definition of souls and the purpose of souls is not consistently explained. Every Earther we questioned about the nature of souls gives a slightly different interpretation which leads us to believe that Earthers do not actually know what or who they are. They have beliefs about souls but no hard evidence.

As determined by us after extensive research into this subject an OE concluded that these entities Earthers call souls do exist and that they are found within every Earther. They are best explained as a race of non-physical energy beings that invest themselves in humans so they can experience physical pleasures and activities which are not available to them in their non-physical existence. Curiously, these non-physical beings who partner with Earthers are also said to believe in a supreme being that they call by several names, such as The Divine One, or The Creator. Humans cannot directly feel these energy beings inside them, since they are not physical and there is therefore nothing to "feel" but somehow, they share a sense that this being, this soul, is there. The great thinkers on Shonak have theorized that the Plus-Five human, evolving as it did so close to the "Plus-Six" realm of non-physical energy, have an innate ability to sense things no Shonakian ever can or will. Since Shonak exists at the slowest of all physical vibrations, we do not dream or pray or feel there is anything but physical existence. This gives us the emotional distance to research this Plus-Five phenomenon and arrive at an unemotionally derived assessment.

We long ago asked ourselves if these energy beings were also present in Shonakians, "feeling" everything we feel, see, and hear. We concluded that we did not have such beings inside us because we do not share the same thoughts or feelings about this Earthers have. We did wonder if this was because of our very low native vibration but since there is no way to determine if this is the case we have thought not.

For Earthers, though, it is different. We know, for example, that early legends from oral Earther histories and early writings about observing "the gods" stem from Shonak's early public use of phase suits and bots of all kinds. We could appear and disappear as we phased in and out of their vibration and Plus-Five Base was not always careful to conceal themselves when doing this. We used phase ships indiscriminately in those times because there was no thought or concern what the natives would think of us. Much like an Earther zoo keeper does not care if the animals see them as they go about their business. They don't care what the animals think of them. Their only concern is for their own safety and the health and safety of the animals under their care. Shonakians had much the same thoughts and concerns when going about their business on pre-technical Plus-Five.

When we visited them on Plus-Five we could

also appear in any form and in any dress we chose for any situation and the native Earthers naturally assumed we were their gods, or in fact, sometimes came to believe in their gods because of what they saw us do. This was before they had technology or scientific understanding of any kind and of course they needed some way to explain sightings of our people. They invented so-called gods and goddesses and monsters to explain what they saw. Shonakians and our bots in anti-grav phase suits flying around and appearing and disappearing in the course of their duties was magic to them. They explained these sightings in the only ways they knew how – it was "the work of the gods." Over time, the creative minds of their story tellers, eager to entertain family and other audiences, embellished these tales to make them even more dramatic and enjoyable.

When Emerald Bon was still a Gold, he famously interacted with the proto-Hopi Earther Atsa. That relationship became the classic case in support of our thesis. Bon was able to use bots which appeared as gods, or Kachinas, to Atsa and his people. Shonakians and their bots at Plus-Five Base could fly, appear and disappear, change their shape, create dragons and huge eagles to fly them from place to place, things no human was capable of. That had to be the gods at work, right?

In 306097/-950 UAY a supposed "real god" famously appeared to Bon and Atsa, and the miraculously assembled leadership of both Shonak and Plus-Five. The "god" lectured them on the nature of the Universe. This event provided much evidence of these aliens and OE determined that this event was one of the clearest manifestations to date. He concluded that this being was one of these alien life forms, without native physical substance, and which is vastly superior to Shonak in its use of technology. He concluded that there is nothing supernatural about them, they are just fellow travelers seeking their pleasures where they might, not unlike Shonakians. While they experience Earther lives from the inside, we on Shonak experience Earther lives from the outside. Ironically, we see a great similarity between souls and Shonakians in their use of humans. Souls partner with humans to experience the five senses they don't have, and never will. Shonakians watch humans to experience the emotions and senses of Earthers that Shonakians don't have and never will.

Shonak is looking forward to the time when we can have an open and direct communication with this race of energy beings. The present arrangement, laundering our relationship with them through Earth humans, is inefficient and ineffective.

The title of the diary in the narrative below is, "A Fourth Primary Color." That alludes to the difficulty in discussing a topic for which the audience has no frame of reference, and no possibility of getting one. How can you fully explain music to the deaf or color to the blind?

This collection of oral pronouncements collected over a period of time by a variety of static and dynamic bots carry the spiritual musings of Kuivato, a proto-Hopi holy man near the end of his life. He is famous in Vid-Watch history for his work with Emerald Bon while Bon was a new Gold, when he was Eldest of Plus-Five Base. Kuivato was mentor to the young Atsa, later chief of this primitive tribe, and to his father, and indeed to the village, and in a sense to Gold Bon as well, since none of them had the wisdom or frame of reference to think of them without his help. Kuivato's stated intention was to pass along some of his wisdom to whomever might benefit by it. His words were collected over the space of several S-Rots as he spoke with himself out loud and with his people on these matters. This diary is a follow-on to the Shonakian perspective about the soul you have just heard. This diary provides an Earther perspective on the same subject. It is an example of deep Earther thinking of a spiritual nature and carries a Native American holy man's musing on the relationship of humans to their souls, their alien within. Kuivato is a resident of what his people call their Fourth World, which is a holy distinction given to their chosen living space in an inhospitable location in the high desert regions of the American Southwest, USNA. He lived a thousand S-Rots before +1 UAY. As noted in the previous diary, Shonak has concluded that souls are nothing more than alien beings of perhaps pure energy, without physical substance, who invade Earther natives for purely voyeuristic purposes. They seek to experience the five senses since they do not have them at their level of existence. This diary gives a different opinion, an Earther opinion, which may be of some value to Shonakian scholars interested in the topic. This diary contains a compilation of the things Kuivato said to his people when instructing them on the nature of the human-soul relationship.

Diary from the Earther Perspective. "I'm sure it comes as no surprise that the differences between humans and their inner spirits are profound, but there are also things in common. As you listen to me your inner spirit is also listening to me. You will have perceptions of what I say and so will your inner spirit but comparing what you hear and what your inner spirit hears is like comparing what you hear with what your pet dog hears. It is unlikely that both you and your dog will think of my words and the thoughts they convey in the same way or take away the same message. In fact, and of course, your dog won't understand the words at all, but may listen to them. Your inner spirit, on the other hand, will hear and understand. Not that these inner spirits or souls are smarter than humans they just have a more relevant perspective in certain areas. We humans can speak more truth on the taste of a warm, fresh-baked loaf of corn bread than any inner spirit can, even though they share our experience eating the bread. Its limitation comes from the fact that it tastes the bread indirectly, through you. Your soul, or inner spirit, on the other hand, can speak more truth on the nature of Creation even though it may share something of it with you. That sharing with you is like your "sharing" the bread with it; it is an indirect and subtle form of communication that is very easy to confuse and mislead. Most humans only hear the voice of their inner spirit on rare occasions and even then it sounds like someone shouting from a great distance, something heard dimly, above the wind. And, because we must consider ourselves the lesser relation when discussing spiritual matters, our souls talk to us like we talk to our dogs. No harm in that, just the way it is. And, naturally, this conversation, if that's what it is, will be full of misunderstandings and misinterpretations. Like if you try to explain the process by which you made that loaf of bread to your dog. Your dog simply will not get it; wrong language and no relevant frame of reference. It is the same with us and our inner spirits. We do not have any relevant frame of reference for life above the physical plane. Our dog can't "get" the human perspective. You can't "get" the spirit's perspective. And your inner spirit can't "get" your perspective either, at least not perfectly. Nothing sinister about it. Again, just the way it is.

As a result, we humans can discuss spiritual matters intelligently and with significant understanding only insofar as our spiritual self interacts with our physical self. This is how holy men and other people with psychic ability grasp non-physical experiences. It is however a far cry from understanding them in any meaningful sense given the full extent of such things. The physical planes make up only some five percent of Creation so the ninety-five percent beyond our direct senses are simply beyond our ability to fully understand. That is very likely a permanent condition.

We humans tend to assume our inner spirits have great intelligence and wisdom and understanding of all things in Creation but the truth is they were born just as ignorant as we were. They have had to learn to understand their situation and accommodate to it, or not, just as we have. In this regard the only difference is the length of time our souls have been pursuing their lives when compared to individual humans, or even to humanity collectively. Humans or what passes for humans have been around on Earth for two million or so years. Souls have been around since the beginning of Everything. Then there is the issue of mortality for humans. While each of us has been partnered with our inner spirit every day of our lives it is nothing close to what our souls have lived through. Of course, the root of this difference lies in the fact that our souls live forever, and we do not. When we "remember" a past life it is our inner spirit doing the remembering, not us. Our past life continuity is completely the province of the soul. All the people our souls have been partnered with before us are gone and returned to dust, but the memory of their lives is still perfectly tucked away in the memory of these souls. They are our continuity with the past in a way that no lesson of history can be.

It must be said that this is not a free ride for our souls. Souls pay a price for partnering with humans, or with anything else on the physical plane of existence. They are not native to this plane. Their plane of existence is at vibrations above the physical. Physical things simply lose cohesion at those vibrations, so they don't exist there. Our thoughts, which are not physical, do live out there but our bodies do not. For an inner spirit to partner with something on the physical plane they have to reduce their vibration sufficiently to perceive us and merge with our vibration. When they first learn how to do this it is not perfectly done but they get better at it over time. And the better they get at riding the physical plane the more enamored they become of it. And why not? They do not actually become physical, so they retain their immortality. They also do not actually feel what we feel but what they have is the next best thing. It is confusing to them at first. They can "feel" gravity, the fact that there is an up and down, the fact that there is hot and cold, the fact that there is pain, but also pleasure. In time they learn to feel our pain, our joys, our fears, our doubts, our loves and our hates. And so some of them get a little intoxicated by it. So while they do not become physical they can "dumb themselves down" enough to experience what we experience, admittedly with a certain level of removal. They can feel our pain by "feeling" our thoughts of pain but of course they cannot experience physical pain themselves. They can experience our pleasures in the same way. Finally, they experience our death in the same way, by experiencing ours, but of course they cannot themselves die. They can experience our loves, our hates, our triumphs and our failures. They can know what it is to be rich or poor, smart or dim-witted, athletic or sedentary, healthy or sick, beautiful or ugly, talented or not so much. But they only know these things through us and not directly themselves.

Having said all that, the question remains - why do souls do this at all? The answer is that souls all have the same ultimate goal. They must learn enough by whatever means at their disposal to abandon hate in favor of love regardless of the provocation to do otherwise as evidenced by their every thought, word, and deed. This includes *our* every *human* thought, word, and deed when they are partnered with one of us. And here lies the great message about the human-inner spirit partnership: Eventually the souls who partner with humans decide that it is time to move onward and upward in their individual journeys towards reunification with the Divine. These are the more experienced and advanced souls who have chosen to actually *accept responsibility* for what their human partners do. On the other side of this coin are the many souls, if not even most souls, who do not care about what we do. They are having a grand time with us and it really doesn't matter to them what we get up to. And as for us, the human partners, we mostly remain ignorant about our inner spirit and what it is doing or trying to do. Some do believe they have a inner spirit but even so, the vast majority of humanity just goes about its business with the inner spirit along for the ride.

Souls often do their best to help their partners achieve "goodness" but two things stand in their way. First, Free Will is an absolute and cannot be interfered with. So when the human decides to do something bad, there is little the souls can do about it other than work with the conscience of the human and seek to limit these bad choices by helping the human decide not to make them in the first place. Secondly, the inner spirit is hampered by the fact that there is precious little knowing communication between human and soul. This is an area which needs improvement, and which can actually improve, and it is my job to make sure you know about this problem.

Reaching our souls is easy. They are aware of all we do and all we think, all day, every day. There is not a moment where we have any privacy from our souls. Conversely, though, we humans do a terrible job getting any direct information from our souls. What passes for our conscience gets messages, but we mostly ignore them if they do not agree with what we want to do. In our dreams we get the most messages but so many people do not remember their dreams, and when they do, they have no idea what they mean.

The old saying, "The devil on my left shoulder and the angel on my right" pretty much covers what we all experience. There is no evil spirit, by the way, only the one we create for ourselves. "The Evil One made me do it" is simply an excuse we use to explain away something we would not like to take the blame for. We also know right from wrong and it is wrong to attribute that to any angel. While angels do exist, in a manner of speaking, there is no reason to suggest we need our inner spirit to tell us right from wrong. The very large gray area in between what is clearly wrong and clearly right is where the inner spirit tries to help. The amount of influence they have is inconsistent. It depends on the rational maturity of the human they are partnered with. Sociopaths will not listen to their souls and sensitive, mature adult humans do not need to. Most of us, again, lay somewhere in between.

Many times, I have tried to explain this to my people and have concluded that it is like trying to explain a fourth primary color. Souls would know this color but it does not exist on the physical plane, where these ranges of vibrations won't support it. How then do they convey it to us? The answer is they can't. No amount of desire will make it so. Thought creation might be a way to achieve it but when the vibration that is the fourth primary color attempts to enter the consciousness of a human partner it loses its identity and dissipates like a forgotten memory. And so it is with information about the Soul, our inner spirit partners, who can no more explain themselves to us than we can explain our Kachinas to our dog. We are simply left with an understanding for our People of The Fourth World; work hard, place love above hate, and care for the Earth and all its people, and always do our best.

ABOUT THE AUTHOR

Dennis retired from the Army in 2000, after thirty years, and five wars; Vietnam and the First Gulf War, The Cold War, the Global War on Terror, and the peace keeping effort in the Balkans. He is a retired Army Colonel, a combat wounded veteran, and in spite of his first book, A Million Monkeys, not at all religious. The first part of his life was entirely conventional. He grew up in a non-religious Navy family, living around the country and around the world, until his father retired in Phoenix, Arizona. Dennis was in the seventh grade.

After graduation from Arizona State University Dennis went into the Army via the RoTC program and his first tour of duty was in Vietnam where he was wounded by enemy mortar fire. He served for thirty years, more than half of which was overseas, as noted above. In addition, he was the US Army's first **"Cyber Cop"** and when he retired in 2000, he went to work in the cyber security business. After the tragedy of 9/11, he was hired by the Massachusetts Port Authority to run the security program overseeing three airports and the city's seaports.

As he got older things in his life changed. He married an accomplished artist with a PsyD who was also ordained as a minister in the Church of Spiritualism. He became a Reiki Master and studied spiritual things while being **"coached"** through the contents of A Million Monkeys, the Real Story Behind Genesis and The Meaning of Life. It was an odd sensation for this old soldier to channel a Spirit in writing this book. Dennis found the whole thing difficult to accept but finally translated the thoughts he was given into what you can read yourself.

Dennis was more comfortable accepting his role as Narrator of the story, not the originator, and as a result wrote the book in the second person, since it is essentially a lecture to Humanity by a Spirit describing itself only as a **"Super-Soul of some magnitude."** It may be seen as religious as it covers religious subjects, but it should not be seen as the enemy of established religions. They are what they are and as creations of Mankind, are understandably flawed however well-intentioned. If you are looking for the answers, that is, the actual answers to *Genesis and the Meaning of Life*, this is the book you need to read.

The second book, *The Crown of Happenstance*, completes the story from *A Million Monkeys* but is set in a conventional Science Fiction/Fantasy story. That book relates the interaction of the planet Shonak with that of Earth, around about 1000 BCE. The reader is introduced to the cousin planet Shonak, which is an alternate reality version of Earth. The people who evolved there are totally different from natives of Earth, in pretty much every way that matters. No money, no sex, no politics, no relaxation, no gourmet food, no alcohol, no disease, no anger, no love, no families, no religion—just work.

One of their most accomplished citizens is given the task of finalizing their mission on Earth, which they call PlusFive, and he sets about it with the help of a proto Hopi named Atsa. Together they constitute a formidable team, each seeking to further their own agenda by finding and exploiting The Crown of Happenstance, which is said to confer god-like powers on whoever wears it.

The Third book, It's About Time, is about that same notable Shonakian, Gold Bon, and his mission to answer nearly imponderable questions about the nature of Time itself. Along the way he develops a strong connection
with the now modern Earth, introducing them to Shonak and using Shonak's superior technology to help Earth cope with crime, overpopulation, pollution, and the like. The true, and benign agenda of Shonak on Earth is simply watching Earthers go about their daily lives. Shonakians, whose lives are full but boring, find Earth Watching to be hugely entertaining. To them we are large, hairy, sweaty, violent people who do, say, and think things no Shonakian would ever do, say, or think.

To provide the fullest measure of infotainment feeds from Earth, the Shonakians have put millions of "bots" around the planet, some looking like dogs or cats, eagles, mice, or cockroaches. The most intrusive, however, are the ones that replicate humans in every possible way. Using their vast fleet of surveillance collectors, Shonak has turned Earth into a giant cultural theme park, or zoo, for their amusement. In the end, Bon deals with their complex relationship with Earth and finally makes peace with it.

The fourth book, Bot Diaries, is a compilation of bot collection efforts, thoroughly researched by the various
vid-watch clubs on Shonak, to trace some of the more obscure images they have collected. One such "diary" traces the location of the Thirty Pieces of Silver that were paid to Judas Escariot to betray Jesus Christ. Watch for this to come out later in 2020.

ABOUT HIS BOOKS

THE SHONAK SERIES

THE CROWN OF HAPPENSTANCE on its surface this book is about a search for something that may or may not even exist. It is known by many names but the most common is The Crown of Happenstance, and it is rumored to confer god-like powers on whoever wears it. Many rich and powerful rulers on Earth in 1000 BCE are after this Crown for all the obvious reasons, chief of which is to dominate every other ruler who is looking for it. But they are not the only people looking for this Crown. A brilliant race of people from another version of Earth have heard stories of it and what it can do and they also want it. These people, from a very old race of technocrats, already have, through science, what the people of Earth would call god-like powers. They want the Crown for what their science cannot provide—a way of visiting and using the magic of the non-physical parts of Creation. They dream of this Crown giving them the ability to usethoughtcreation to further advance their civilization. These visitors to this Earth are from Shonak, and have established an outpost on Earth to conduct the reconnaissance necessary to find the Crown. During the sixteen hundred years they have been on Earth they have not found it, or even any clues as to where it may be found. Some of their deep thinkers theorize that the short-lived people of Earth have possibly invented stories about this Crown to give people a ray of hope against their decidedly dangerous and difficult lives. Frustrated at their lack of progress in finding it, or anything else of use to Shonak, they have sent their go-to-guy Bon to bring the mission on Earth to successful conclusion. Bon finds young

Atsa, a native of Earth, to help him find the Crown. Atsa lives in a Pueblo village in the Desert Southwest. The joint adventures of Bon and Atsa become legend and at the end of their time together both can claim a measure of success. While they pursue the Crown they are under the constant scrutiny of another race entirely. Not of this Earth, or Shonak, this third party might rightly claim they are children of the Universe. They are alternately called "spirits" or even "souls". They share an interest in the search for the Crown of Happenstance but they see it in a totally different way. And in the end, it is their vision that really matters.

A MILLION MONKEYS

Dennis Treece explains the way this material came to him then narrates the unfolding story of how it all works, how life works, how death works, what human suffering is all about and why it is so common. In the telling, this book provides the answers to life's most fundamental questions Ever wonder what you are here for, what life is all about? Not just your life, but everybody's? How did it all begin and why? Most people accept that they have a soul but what is the nature of the human/soul partnership? What do you get out of it, and what does the soul experience and learn from it? What are souls, anyway? Who are they? Keep reading. You will learn the true nature of Heaven and Hell, what happens when we die, and what the Divine Plan is all about. All that and more. This book is a must-read for everyone who claims a piece of the human condition.